Notes to any offended sensitive reader:

1) If you were to go down to the docks and listen to the uneducated fishermen of Boston, New York, San Francisco, Galway, Liverpool or London (or a squad of Marines) talking to each other, they would hardly sound like a lot of altar boys or novices in a seminary. It's highly unlikely that the fishermen of Bethsaida were any different.

2) Jesus was a man's man, not some goodie-two-shoes. He bled, was hungry, got sick, had toothaches, lost his temper, enjoyed a good meal and wine, and was tempted just like all normal men. He also couldn't have made it without a good sense of humor.

3) Men use nicknames. In my years of service and civilian life, I was never once called 'James', but always 'Jim" or 'Big Jim' ....or worse! Even Jesus nicknamed Simon.

So, here we go!

Liebe mensch gmbh wien, Maria Himmelfahrt 2019

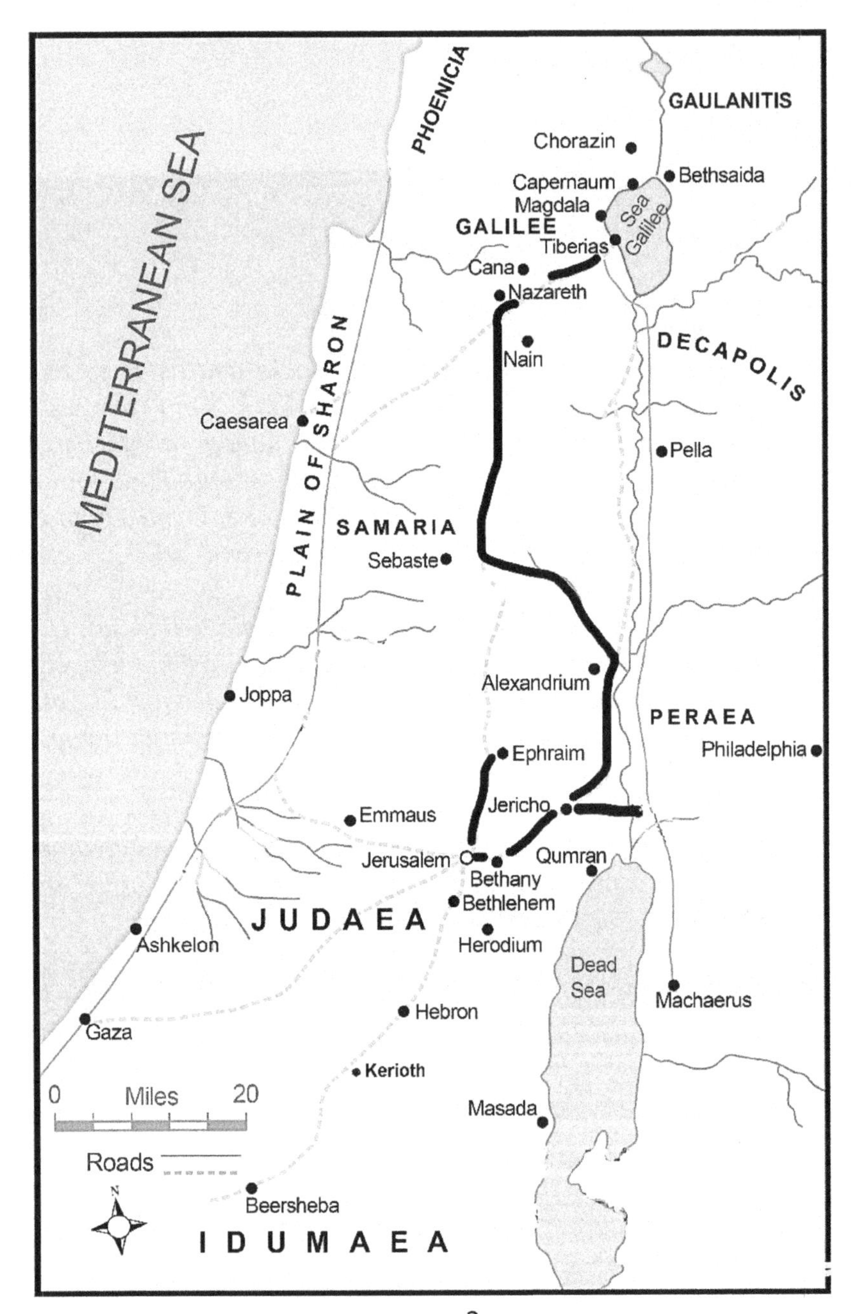
MEDITERRANEAN SEA
PHOENICIA
GAULANITIS
Chorazin
Capernaum
Bethsaida
Magdala
GALILEE
Sea Galilee
Tiberias
Cana
Nazareth
Nain
DECAPOLIS
PLAIN OF SHARON
Caesarea
Pella
SAMARIA
Sebaste
Alexandrium
Joppa
PERAEA
Ephraim
Philadelphia
Jericho
Emmaus
Jerusalem
Qumran
Bethany
Bethlehem
JUDAEA
Ashkelon
Herodium
Dead Sea
Machaerus
Gaza
Hebron
Kerioth
0 Miles 20
Masada
Roads
Beersheba
N
IDUMAEA

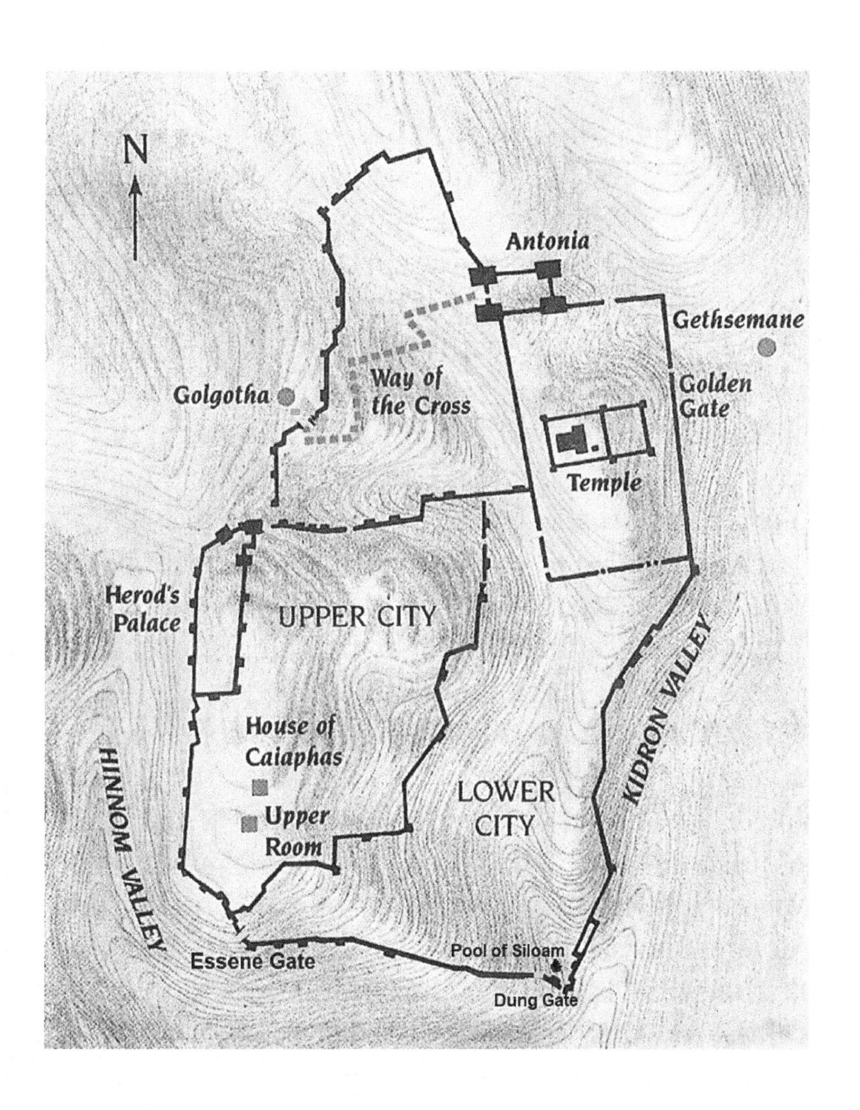
N
Antonia
Gethsemane
Golden Gate
Way of the Cross
Golgotha
Temple
Herod's Palace
UPPER CITY
House of Caiaphas
Upper Room
LOWER CITY
KIDRON VALLEY
HINNOM VALLEY
Essene Gate
Pool of Siloam
Dung Gate

Chapter 1

(Despair)

Expelled from the High Priest's villa, he stumbled aimlessly through garbage cluttered back alleys and congested streets, bumping his way through the passersby. His normally combed brown hair was hanging over his eyes; eyes that had a wild look to them, but he didn't seem aware of it. His normal fastidious appearance was gone, replaced by a disheveled enough look to be noticed by some of the pedestrians. Oh God, what had he done?! A thousand thoughts were running helter-skelter through his head when he stumbled over a little girl knocking her to the ground. She started to cry. He stared down dumbly at her teary eyes, confused and bewildered. He wanted to say he was sorry but nothing came out.

"Watch where you're going you stupid drunk!" Picking up the little girl in his arms, the angry father shoved the unsteady stranger with his free hand, sending him sprawling to the cobblestones. The stranger looked up at the man standing over him. Reaching into his purse proffered a silver denarius. The father angrily slapped the coin from his hand, sending it rolling towards curious onlookers.

"Keep your damned money!"

A young man picked up the coin and handed it back to the stranger who began trembling, tears streaming down his face. He rolled over and struggled to rise, but his legs buckled under him and he dropped to his knees.

(Denarius)

Rocking back and forth on his haunches, he mumbled,

"Dear Master please forgive me. Help me Lord, help me Lord, help me Lord. Please Lord, please Lord. Please Lord, help me."

It felt as if his heart had been ripped from his chest. Tears streamed down his cheeks as mucus dribbled from his nostrils, over his mustache and into his beard. The passersby carefully circumvented the abnormal appearing person slumped on cobbles assuming him to be either drunk or perhaps demented. A few thought him diseased and gave him an even wider berth. He was startled by a hand clasping his shoulder. It was a ragged teenager.

"Are you all right?"

A primitive moan escaped his lips as he looked up at the boy, dazed and confused. The boy took him by the arm and helped him to his feet.

"Can I bring you somewhere? Is there someone who looks after you?"

He shook his head no, then grasped the boy's hand. Wiping his nose on the sleeve of his cloak, he looked at the youth and murmured,

"Thank you.....and please pray for me......Please pray for my soul."

With that, he once again headed in the direction of the Essene Gate *(See map on page 3)*. Somewhere along the way, he had lost a sandal, but in his confused state of mind didn't seem to notice. Working his way through the congested city gate, he was unaware of the traffic of donkeys, carts, camels and their raucous drivers. Once beyond the towering limestone walls of the city, instead of following the contour of the road south towards Bethlehem, he crossed over the first stone fence he ran into. Beyond it was a field through which he wandered aimlessly. It was barley and nearly ripe. The early afternoon sun beat down fiercely, covering his face with sweat. At the far side of the field, he finally gave up and slumped down at the base of an olive tree, emotionally and physically exhausted.

He was twenty-five years old and had wept only twice since he was seven. First, when his mother died. She never failed to kiss him goodnight, even when she became sick. The second time was one dark unforgettable night two years ago when his only friend Aaron died in his arms, wounded when he and five other Zealots had ambushed and killed three drunken legionnaires….damned little Roman bastards despoiling his beloved homeland and desecrating the City of David. Now he sat in despair, his mind in a turmoil. Oh God, what had he done? What had he been thinking? A feeling of total hopelessness overwhelmed him. Oh Master, I'm so sorry. Can you ever forgive me? What in my stupid life have I ever done right? Nothing! He sobbed. He was beyond mercy, beyond redemption, beyond all hope. He lay on his side in a fetal position. He thought about what the Master had taught them about forgiveness. But he was beyond being forgiven. He had sold his soul to the devil…..betrayed the most wonderful human he'd ever known. How can I ever expect him to forgive me? Oh God, what have I done? He buried his face in the dirt and let out a wail of despair. What was the use? Just give up! He whispered, hoping that in the stillness his Lord, God, and Savior would hear him.

"Please Master have mercy on me...Please forgive your worthless servant."

He looked up into an empty sky and felt lost. The pounding of his heartbeat beat in his ears.

"Why must you die Master, why? You're the savior of the world. You can't die. Especially not that way! Why are you letting them do this?... just stop them,... please."

He had witnessed the horrific crucifixion of a tough fellow Zealot he knew named Eben-Ezer. It was the cruelest death the bloody Romans could dream up. Eben had lasted almost two days! The kindest thing one could have wished for poor Eben was a quick death. Of course, that was the whole idea of these cruel, merciless, idol-worshiping Gentiles and their bloody procurator. As a final insult, after Eben had at last died, they threw his corpse out on the Gehenna Valley garbage heap for the feral dogs to tear apart and devour. It was forbidden for his friends or relatives to bury him.

(Eben-Ezer)

"Oh Master Jesus..." he sobbed, *"What have I done to you? How can you ever forgive me? You, the kindest man I've ever known."*

It was hopeless. He was lost....beyond forgiveness.

"I wasn't even able to say I'm sorry. He couldn't hear me with everyone yelling. All I was able to do was wave, like some idiot. Oh God, what have I done? Oh God forgive me."

But there was no place to run to,.....no place to hide. He stopped in the middle of the field to catch his breath between sobs. He was bound for Hell. An ancient Psalm[1] flitted across his bewildered mind:

I am sunk in the abysmal swamp
Where there is no foothold.
I have reached the watery depths,
And the flood overwhelms me.

Getting to his knees, he tried to explain to the Master who wasn't there.

"I tried to tell them it was all a misunderstanding, but they just smirked at me. They're all hypocrites. You even said so yourself. You were always right....I was always wrong. Now you, my one and only friend, my mentor by now are probably dying. Why did you let them? That's all I want to know."

His tears blurred his vision and fell on his folded hands.

---

[1] Psalm 69

"All I was trying to do was change things you know. Couldn't anyone see that?"

He had followed Jesus for over two years and borne witness to the true nature of the man. His kindness, strength, and truth inspired most, but those in power felt threatened. Wasn't he here to liberate God's chosen people from their bloody Roman oppressors? What if that wasn't his intention at all? What have I done? Sentenced a good man to die. All he and his fellow Zealots had ever wanted was to take up arms and resist. Resist until the final invader had been driven from their shores as Judah Maccabeus had done; to defend the poor and the helpless women and children. Wasn't that the path the Master was on….love God and your neighbor?

"Oh dear God, be merciful to me, the worst of all sinners, betrayer of your son. I'm sorry. Please forgive me. Forgive me, oh forgive me!"

A ladder leaned against the tree where he lay. A few feet away laying on the ground was a donkey's halter. In a moment of utter despair, he knew what had to be done. Throwing the halter straps around a sturdy branch, he tied off the makeshift noose and climbed the ladder.

"Master, I'm so sorry for all I have done. Please forgive me!"

….and with that, **Judas stepped off the ladder!….**and the other sandal fell off.

It was about the ninth hour.[2] Had he waited just a few moments longer, he might have felt the earth tremble, and looking north, observed the sky turn ominously black, and heard the rumble of thunder over the northeast section of the city.

[2] Roman daytime was twelve hours. At Passover time, dawn was around 6 a.m. The 1st hour therefore was 7 a.m., the 6th hour noon, and the ninth hour 3 p.m.

Chapter 2

(A few weeks earlier)

Jesus had been preaching in the synagogue at Sepphoris[3] and they were now heading back towards Capernaum and the lake. It was afternoon and as usual, by then, they had become strung out along the road in groups of twos and threes with the wearier and ones with blisters bringing up the rear. Breakfast that morning had consisted of a bowl of tasteless gray gooey barley gruel, a cup of well water, and a handful of figs. They had been proselytizing in the vicinity of the western end of the Jezreel Valley and hadn't had a decent meal in days. Except for Jesus, they were all in their mid-twenties and forever hungry. At least at the lake, they could get fish. Passing through a barley field, some were chewing on the kernels, chaff and all. Levi[4] was complaining,

"Lentil stew with onions, garlic, and peas; bean stew with onions, garlic and leeks; pea stew with onions and garlic! What does a man have to do to have a bit of meat once in a while?"

"Be a rich a Publican like yourself," replied Thomas.

"Correction, formerly rich.....and now hungry," retorted Levi.

---

[3] 4 miles due north of Nazareth

[4] Mathew

Andrew goaded Judas who was walking just ahead of him,

"Hey Moneybags, how about loosening up that purse of yours and giving the women an extra shekel or two to buy some real food for a change?"

Andrew didn't like Judas. If you asked him why, he most likely wouldn't be able to tell you. It was probably just a difference in personalities. Feelings were apparently mutual as Judas irritably barked back.

*"**That's 'Treasurer' to you**!.....and if you don't like the way I'm handling our funds, go complain to the Master and the job is yours."*

*"Oh excuse me '**Mister Treasurer'.** Well, I'm a 'fisherman'. You know, someone who actually produces something for a living, not a pen pusher. All we want is a couple shekels for real food."*

"Look Andy, you know as well as I do that we live on unreliable contributions mostly from rich people and Publicans the Master is friends with. So, we need to scrimp on our limited resources in case he decides we go to Jerusalem for the Passover. Remember, if we go, we'll be on the road for over a week and need every mite[5] just to eat, even if we can't afford an inn and must camp out. Money doesn't grow on trees you know."

"Maybe if you didn't stash a little away once in a while for yourself, we'd have enough!"

---

[5] Smallest coin

"Look pal! If you're accusing me of stealing, let's go see Jesus right now. I'm not taking any more crap from you or your big brother! *I can account for every damned mina (50 shekels) that Centurion from Capernaum donated, as well those of that official whose twelve-year-old daughter the Master seemed to bring back to life. That also goes for the shekels the women (Joana, Mary from Magdala, and Susanna) have been contributing. Go ahead and ask them! And speaking of stealing, did I or did I not observe the man to whom you and your brother* ***'lent'*** *your boat to while we were last away, handing you money...* ***'rent'*** *was it? Somehow Big-shot, I don't seem to recall you contributing that to our funds. Maybe the Master would appreciate hearing you explain about that. What do you think?"*

"Calm down. Don't get your balls in an uproar. I'm just complaining that we're all sick and tired of lentil and onion stews and that lousy barley garbage you call bread. What about some decent wheat bread? By the way, I notice you don't object to enjoying the fish we ignorant, hicks catch whenever we are near the lake."

Young John who was up ahead heard the part about food and called back over his shoulder, making the mistake of inadvertently resurrecting a subject that had almost caused a recent mutiny.

"I'll tell you one thing. Once the Master runs off the Romans and makes me Tetrarch of Galilee, I plan

to have meat every night....a nice succulent lamb, or maybe even a fatted calf once in a while....and what do you guys think of honey cakes for dessert? Won't that be living?"

Thomas angrily hollered,

"Hey, listen to me kid! *The rest of us take a dim view of you and your brother thinking you can lord it over us when the Master gets to be king.....and we don't appreciate your mom asking the Master for you two to be his seconds-in-command. Don't get me wrong, your mother is a nice lady an all, and we all appreciate her doing our wash and cooking her* ***'wonderful'*** *stews. But women should keep their big noses out of politics. The day I have to take orders from you kid, is the day I say* ***'Leitraot!*** *('Goodbye' in Hebrew). And another thing! When the Master told us about his kingdom, I seem to recall him saying we'd be sitting on* ***twelve*** *thrones,* ***not three!*** *He made no mention of you ruling a third of the country and your big brother another third,* ***get it?!****"*

A couple of angry voices seconded the motion. The twelve seemed to be always bickering over something or other especially when tired and hungry. But this subject topped the list. The only thing that prevented a second revolt was when Jesus who was up ahead heard them. He had stopped at the side of the road to chat with a ragged beggar and their sharp barbs interrupted him. Since it was about time for a break, and beside the road was a terebinth tree offering its shade and a place to rest, he decided to call a halt. When all were seated, he spoke, trying hard to keep from losing his patience.

(A terebinth tree)

"When will you guys ever learn, eh? How often must I remind you? Sometimes you act a lot like the Pharisees.....want people to be bowing and scraping, making believe you're somehow important. Is that what you want to be, bigshots? You want to wear fancy robes with little bells to let people know you are coming? Is that it? And you John Boy. Do you really think you are more important to me and the Father than the others? What about you Big Jim?....you too? That goes for the lot of you. Do you think that I picked you because you're smarter, holier or better looking than the rest of the men around Galilee? No! I picked you because you're typical decent, everyday men, not afraid to work, who are hardly perfect, but at least try to be

good, though not always succeeding. I've picked you to be my starting team. Oh, and another thing while I'm at it. I've been treating Peter here in a special way. (*Jesus half-joking had nicknamed Simon the 'Rock' mainly because of his dense, stubborn hard-headedness*). *Does that mean he's somehow better than the rest of you? Heck no! He has his flaws like all of us. For one thing, he can't keep his big foot out of his mouth and argues with me about everything, right Peter?* (chuckles). *I chose him because every successful team must have a leader otherwise it falls apart. Every army must have a general or it's defeated. I've told you that I'm not always going to be around, not with Antipas up here and the Sanhedrin out to get me. So, I had to choose one of you as my backup. Maybe I should've picked one of you. But, right or wrong, for better or for worse, Peter was my choice. You all know and respect him. He's the oldest. What are you Peter, twenty-eight? Even when fishing, I noticed he is more-or-less your unspoken boat captain and leader. Look over there a few miles to the south of us at Mt. Tabor. You may remember, and perhaps were a bit peeved, that I only took, Peter, Big Jim, and John Boy along with me. It wasn't that the rest of you didn't count, but rather that I needed my leader there. I also needed a couple of witnesses or you'd never believe what he would someday be free to say he had witnessed*[6]. *And lastly! Just as I wait on you and on the poor beggars and the*

[6] The Transfiguration

sick we come across, so I expect you to wait on each other. So, ***just once in a while****, do me a favor and stop your incessant bickering. Oh, and by the way, this kingdom of mine I keep telling you about, is not of this world, nor will yours be.*

(Mt. Tabor)

When he was done, they all were quiet……and confused. What the heck was that *"....not of this world"* business about? Then Philip lightened the gloom with another of his awful anecdotes. It was about the story of the lion who thought he was more important than the other animals around him.

"There was this lion you see. He was going around the jungle bragging and bullying the other animals. He came to the chimpanzee and roared,

"Chimp, who be da King a da Jungle?!"

"You is lion, you is. Everybody knows dat." replied the frightened chimpanzee.

"I is an don't you fergit it!"

He next came to the hyena who answered the same way. Each animal in turn readily responded to his threatening question the same as the chimp and hyena had,

"You is lion, You is."

All went well until he came to the elephant. The lion demanded,

"Elfant, who be da King a da Jungle?!

Now the elephant had had a bad day. He was tired and to make him even more irritable, he had a painful thorn in his left forefoot. So instead of replying, he angrily wrapped his trunk around the lion, lifted him ten feet in the air, and then **slammed** *him to the ground and sat on him! The stunned lion finally staggered back up to his feet and meekly complained,*

"Hey man, jes cause ya don't know da answer, ain't no reason ta get so mad about it!"

Nathaniel who never got jokes, made matters worse by stupidly asking,

"Are you the elephant Master?"

Andrew the perpetual grouch whom they sometimes referred to as *'Old Sour Puss'* added,

"Phil do us all a favor and keep your stupid jokes to yourself."

(Phil)

Chapter 3

(Philip's joke)

It was late afternoon, and they were all reclining on the grass on the hillside leading down to the lake at Capernaum. As usual, the outsiders Judas the lone non-Galilean and Levi, were off by themselves critiquing the day's events. The two didn't sync too well with the rest of the twelve, especially with the primary clique which according to Judas consisted of the fishermen from the vicinity of Bethsaida and Chorazin *(two miles north of Capernaum)*. This group seemed to consider themselves superior in standing to the others. In their eyes, their precedence with the Master was a matter of seniority, having been selected first. In Judas' and Levi's view, they were nothing more than a gang of rowdy, opinionated, loud-mouthed, uneducated, boorish, provincial hicks. Making up this clique were the *'Bigshot'* himself Simon, *'Old Sour Puss'* Andrew his brother, along with Big Jim and his teenager brother John Boy. Lesser members were Philip, Nathaniel, and Thomas all seven, local fishermen. A second and lesser clique was comprised of the other James and his brothers Thaddeus who was a farmer, and Little Simon who was a Zealot[7]. Levi and Judas made up the last and least clique.

Judas came from Keriot in southern Judea near Hebron and not too far from the border of Idumaea *(see*

---

[7] Members of the underground resistance against the Roman occupiers

map on page 3). He didn't have a particularly happy childhood, especially after his mother died when he was seven. After that there was no affection, certainly not from his father Simon. By nature, he was introverted and had no friend growing up other than Aaron. The only thing he got from his father seemed to be criticism.

"Judas why can't you be more like your brother....and stop going around with a chip on your shoulder feeling sorry for yourself?"

His brother Samuel was two years older and his father's pride and joy. He had everything Judas seemed to lack. Sam was outgoing, friendly, self-confident, the top of his class in Torah School, and was interested in, and of course, would inherit his father's wool business. His father wasn't unhappy when at the age of fifteen, Judas ran away from home with Aaron and the pair joined the Zealots.

Of Jesus' twelve, he as the only non-Galilean. He was clearly an outlander especially with his Judean accent, urban appearance, and better education. To make matters worse, Jesus had assigned him the keeper of their company's purse.

(Judas)

Levi, although coming from Nazareth, was the other outsider having been a Publican *(crooked tax collector)*. Thus it was, that the two sat off by themselves discussing the day's activities. Levi was speaking.

"I wonder what happened to the Master's good humor today. He really seemed irritable. He sure lit into Capernaum, Bethsaida and Chorazin didn't he?.....comparing them as ***worse than Sodom, and***

even Sidon and Tyre[8]*. I'll bet that upset 'our Leader' Big Mouth and the others from Bethsaida."*

"Well, Jesus seems to be having gut aches lately. Have you noticed how he's been rubbing his belly?....probably from worrying over the rumors that both Herod and the Sanhedrin are out to get him. I tell you Levi, it sure as hell would give me ulcers. You wonder why he doesn't cure himself? Anyway, as far as today goes, his irritation might've been those three or four Pharisees with their girlie mannerisms who were trying to trip him up in the synagogue. This town seems to have more than its share of queers. The Master is sure touchy about sexual activities outside of normal marriage."

Levi began chuckling.

"Why? What's so funny?"

"I was just thinking of the story of God being angry with all the queers in Sodom and Gomorrah. Remember how Father Abraham weaseled and haggled God down like a common Jerusalem street vendor, and how God let him get away with it?

Levi began by imitating the low-class Jerusalem street vendor dialect.

"Oy God, if dhere vere 50 good peoples in da zity vould jou be sparing it?"

"And getting away with that trick, he had the chutzpah to try for 40, then 30, then 20, and even 10. Can't you imagine God beginning to grit his teeth?"

---

[8] Pagan Phoenician cities on the northwest coast.

"Can't you see Simon trying to pull that stunt on the Master?" (now it was Judas' turn imitating Simon's local fisherman's dialect)

"Hey Master. If there are ten good people in Bethsaida would you spare it?"(by now both men were chuckling)

"....and telling these guys not to look back, would be like guaranteeing that half of the dummies would end up columns of salt."(more chuckling).

That evening lying around the fire on the beach, Jesus seemed back to his old good-natured self again. Earlier that day before losing his temper in town, he had warned them against falling for phony religious leaders claiming to be personally speaking with God. So, it came as no surprise when Philip with a straight face, began telling them about a prophet.

"There once was this prophet see. His name was Menachem. He traveled from village to village promising to heal the repentant sick, and infirm. One day he came to the little village of Pela. You all know it, the one, across the Jordan in the Decapolis. That evening the townspeople gathered at his tent where after taking up a collection, he began,

"Are dhere any repentant sinners among you vhat vish to being cured?"

A woman raised her hand. He called to her,

"Zo, vhat is you name und affliction?"

She stuttered with a lisp,

"Ma-my na-name ith Th-Thuthanna and I have a th-thpeach 'pediment."

"Zo, come forvard Zusanna und be goink behind da coitain (which was merely a piece of tenting hung over a line stretched between two olive trees). If you are being repentant, I vill cure you. Is dhere anyvone elsz?"

A sturdy middle-aged cripple raised his hand, "I'm Simon the Smithy and I've broken my leg and can no longer work my forge. I wish to be cured."

"Zo, come forvard Simon und be goink behind da coirtain vit Susanna."

The prophet Menachem then prayed and invoked Yahweh to heal these two poor afflicted souls. He then commanded,

"Zo, Simon, trow vone of you crutches over da coirtain."....and a crutch came sailing over. The townspeople all gasped in awe and wonder.

"Zo, now Simon, trow da udder crutch over da coirtain."....and the other crutch flew over. By now the people were almost down on their knees.

"Zo, now Zusanna say somezink."

The wonderstruck townspeople held their breath in anticipation, Then her voice rang out in a studder,

"Th-Thimon the Th-Thmithy juth fell on hith aa-aath!"

Jesus and the others burst out into laughter. Andrew just had a grumpy look on his face. Nathaniel looked puzzled. Jesus said,

"Somebody please explain it to Nate."

Levi could swear he saw by the firelight, a twinkle in the Master's eye as the Master called over to Philip,

"Hey Phil! By any chance, did that faith healing prophet Menachem come from Nazareth? What was it again that young Nate here said when you told him about me?"

Levi looked over at Philip who was sitting directly across the fire from him enjoying himself.

"If my memory serves me right Master, I think young Nate here said, "Whoever heard of anyone with any intelligence ever coming out of Nazareth?" ....something like that."

Nathaniel choked on his piece of fish, but before he could lie his way out, Levi spoke up deliberately '*stirring the pot*',

"Hey! *I resent that remark* ***Bartholomew***[9]*, I come from Nazareth too you know."*

While they were all laughing, Nathaniel finally got a word in edgewise,

"It's all a big lie Master. I didn't say that....well not exactly....and Philip, if you ever tell that story again, I'm gonna belt you in the eye!"

This got them laughing even harder, especially Jesus.

---

[9] Nathaniel was the son of Ptolemy, i.e. Bar Ptolemy or simply Bartholomew

(Jesus)

Chapter 4

(Heading south)

The next day, Jesus told them to pack up, that they were leaving for Jerusalem and the Passover Festival *(see the black line they were to travel on the map on page 3 map)*. In a somber tone, he then said something that disturbed the heck out of them, and what was worse, this wasn't the first time he'd made such a grim prediction.

"We're going up to Jerusalem where they're going to arrest me and then hand me over to the Romans to be crucified. But don't worry though, three days later the Father will raise me back to life."

As he listened to this depressing doom and gloom announcement, Judas glanced over at Jesus' mom who had a heartbreaking look on her normally serene features. This was either the second or third time he had alluded to such an ominous scenario. Did he really mean it, or was it another one of his sometimes cryptic pronouncements? In addition, some of them didn't feel particularly comfortable with his use of the word *"We"* when predicting *'crucifixion'*. If this was a real prophecy, what the hell was in store for the rest of them?! And more to the point, why then were they going there in the first place? Simon apparently felt the same way. As usual, he shot off his mouth with the first thought that entered his head.

"Master if they intend to do as you say, I say we just remain here in peaceful Galilee where except for the Tetrarch, most everyone likes us."

"Peter Peter, must you object to everything I say?"

(Simon)

Jesus' mother backed up Simon,

"Jesus, listen to Simon and your mother. Stay here and keep out of trouble."

"Mom, I'm not twelve-years-old. I don't need you and Peter telling me what to do and not to do. ***Please!"***

"Well all I'm trying to say, is that if you won't listen to your own mother who loves you, then at least consider what your best friend is advising."

"Mom, I can't help but listen to the man. Talking to him is like talking to a rock. So, everyone, let's get on with the move.....you too Mom.....and please get that hurt look off your face. It won't work this time, or tears either."

There were a few chuckles, over that exchange, but by and large, after that, no one said much of anything. There was no more happy banter and laughing. It was a lousy way to start a long journey, switching from lively anticipation to somber brooding following his gloomy prediction.

There were nevertheless one or two exceptions to this sense of gloom and doom, namely Judas and Little Simon. After thinking about it, both found it inconceivable that the Jesus' heavenly father, ***'The Father',*** would ever tolerate a bunch of measly, worthless, insignificant specks down in Jerusalem daring to hurt his son. Heck, if given the power to prevent it, what normal earthly father since Abraham would allow such a thing to happen to his child? Both men like all Zealots, had a burning hatred for all those rich, sanctimonious, collaborating, ass-kissing bastards down there in the City of David.

****

Excluding the curious and sick who followed Jesus wherever he went, there were eighteen in their party heading south. This number included Mary *(Jesus' mother)*, Mary Clopas *(the mother of Thaddeus, the other James, and the other Simon)*, Joana *(the wife of Herod's steward of all people!)*, and Salome *(James' and John's mother)*. On top of that to be packed and loaded, were the pots, pans, water jugs, tents, clothing, belongings, and the three poor donkeys to tote it all.

Their first stop was the little village of Magdala to pick up young Mary *(probably Jesus' most loyal and bravest disciple)* who lived in a nice upper-class house by the lakeshore. Behind her back, the men referred to her as *'the Magdalene' (i.e. the Mary from Magdala)*. Their next stop was at Tiberius where the women bought additional food supplies. Nathan and Philip had volunteered to help the women carry the groceries back to camp. As they sat watching Joana heatedly haggle with a vendor over some price, Philip grinned.

"Nate, do you know why Jewish women prefer husbands that are circumcised?"

"I'll bite, why?"

"Because they always prefer getting things that are 20% off."

"I don't get it."

"That's because you're an idiot. Forget it."

They camped out that night on the slope of Mt. Tabor. Fortunately, the rainy season was just at an end so the weather was dry though still chilly. Curled up in his robe, Nathaniel asked Thomas next to him,

"Tom, what are the lights over there?"

"That's the Village of Nain Nate. We were there last year, and the Master appeared to have brought back to life the son of a poor widow."

"Tell me about it."

"You never heard that story? Well, as we were approaching the town gate, we bumped into a funeral procession that was coming the other way. On their shoulders, they were carrying the corpse in its shroud on a stretcher. It was a young guy. As I recall, I think the only child of a widow. Anyway, Jesus did what he always does when he comes across someone who's brokenhearted. He went over and consoled her and then reaching up, touched the body and it sat up! Well, to say the least, that pretty much shocked the hell out of everyone."

"But he was dead!"

"Everyone seemed to think so, but that's a bit hard to imagine, don't you think? You know, sometimes people are so sick they appear to be dead. I remember when my cousin Yakov and Maryanne had their first baby, Saul. About the third night, the kid was so still they both thought it might be dead. They couldn't see or hear any breathing. So, Yakov pinched it. At that,

the baby let out a howl and cried keeping him up the whole damned night. After that Yakov let 'sleeping dogs lie' so to speak"

"Ya think the Master pinched the dead guy?"

*"Well, he touched him. He's amazing. I can sort of understand him curing sick people...**but cripples and blind people?!...and dead people?** that's something else! He's certainly a prophet. Look at what he did to 'the Magdalene'. She had been running around town screaming obscenities and throwing things at everyone....a real loony case. Then the Master simply talks to her the way he does, and ever since she is more normal than most of us. Like Phil told you after he first met him, we all think Jesus is the Messiah all right."*

"Yeah, and Phil also told him what I said. Phil's an idiot."

Thomas was still chuckling as he fell asleep.

On day #2, the crowd that had been tagging along had thinned out quite a bit. This day they made it as far as the fertile Valley of the Jezreel without any remarkable incident.

The subsequent day, they crossed the Valley and climbed up into the hill country of Samaria. It was in the vicinity of Sebaste that afternoon, that they came upon the lepers. As usual, the youngsters John, Philip, and Nathaniel were ahead of the others when they rounded a bend, and there sitting at the side of the road were these disgusting lepers; ten of them. They rang their little bells as required to warn the oncoming group of travelers to steer clear, and then began begging.

"Strangers, alms for the love of God. We're hungry. Have pity on us."

All that could be seen were their faces and hands.....or more accurately what was left of what were once faces and hands. More than one appeared to be blind or almost so. Some were missing noses, others fingers, and probably toes. A few faces were erupted in some fashion or other, and all appeared sad, bewildered, and emotionally defeated. Holding their noses and covering their mouths, John, Philip, and Nathaniel instinctively retreated to the far side of the road for fear of the commonly held belief of smell and contagion[10]. In a nasal voice, Philip brightened.

"Hey you two, here we go again. The Master can't resist these guys. Watch this. "Shalom gentlemen. Unfortunately, we three are as usual, broke, but, ask that tall fellow right behind us. He's Jesus the prophet from Galilee."

Hearing that, the ten excitedly struggled to their feet and shuffled apparently on damaged feet in the direction of the tall man who had been conversing with a younger, shorter grouchy looking individual. All seemed to clamor out at once,

"Jesus, Master, have pity on us!"

---

[10] Leprosy got a bad rap. There is no odor, contagion, or putrification!

Despite their frightening reputation and appearance, Jesus went right up to them and began conversing in a low friendly voice and even worst, laying his hands on their heads. The rest of the company including Simon *'their leader'*, judiciously hung back a safe, commonsense distance.

After a bit Nathaniel heard the Master say,

"Go back into town to the priest for ritual cleansing." ....and with that, the ten headed off in the direction of Sebaste....but this time, instead of shuffling, they had a pronounced spring to their gait.

Not too long afterward, a man came running after them from the direction of town and breathlessly threw himself at Jesus' feet thanking him. John, Nathaniel, and Philip were standing close by staring at the man. He was dressed like the lepers they had just met, and even had the little warning bell. But his face and hands were as fresh and healthy-looking as theirs. They heard Jesus inquire,

"And where are the others?"

"I don't know Lord, but I came back to thank you and may God bless you." The man had a Samaritan accent.

Jesus just shook his head, sighed, and muttered to himself,

"Cured of their horrible nightmare disease and only one in ten is grateful. It all seems so hopeless."

Philip whispered to Nate and John Boy,

"See, what did I tell you. He's gone and done it again, and no matter how you look at it, it's sure no trick."

A puzzled Thomas who with them added,

"How the heck does he do that?"

When evening approached, they stopped for the night at a caravanserai at the small Samaritan village of Beth Dagon a short distance east of Sebaste. Simon and Big Jim approached the Innkeeper for permission to bed down for the night in the courtyard and obtain food and access to the well. John was tagging along with Judas who was also there in case there was a fee to be haggled over and paid. The man gruffly inquired,

"Where are you people from?"

"Tiberias."

"Where are ya goin?"

Before Big Jim could stop him, Simon replied,

"Jerusalem".

"What for?"

Simon had a short fuse to begin with, and this guy rudely asking questions was beginning to get on his nerves.....which in Simon's case, wasn't particularly hard to do.

"Passover, why?"

"Well, we don't have any space for you here, so be on your way."

"What do ya mean no space? Your courtyard is practically empty!"

"No space for any damned Judeans! End of discussion. On yer way, cuz yer not staying here!"

It was a good thing that the man turned on his heel and walked away because Simon had to restrain Big Jim who had been about to *'bust him one on the chops'!*

Big Jim complained,

"Damnit Simon why didn't ya just tell the son-of-a-bitch we were going to Jericho and let it go at that."

Simon just growled something unprintable. When they reported back, Jesus too was angry. But what upset him even more, was when Big Jim proposed,

"Master, what say we wipe this town off the map with fire and brimstone, just like the Father did at Sodom."

Jesus just stared at him in disbelief. They were perfectly serious! It was as if they hadn't heard a word he'd said over the past three years. John Boy made it worse.

"It's a great idea Jesus. Leave this dump of a town in smoking ruins, and after that, there won't be a village or town in the whole country that'll dare not to convert to whatever you say. I say let's do it!"

Judas hearing this also found the idea appealing, but knowing Jesus, unlike Jim and his kid brother, knew when to keep his mouth shut. Poor Jesus thought,

"Good grief Father. You sent me down here to convert the whole world, and I can't even convert these twelve numbskulls! Maybe I should've picked twelve farmers. So much for loving thy neighbor!"

Before going to sleep that night, Judas was off alone with Little Simon and asked him,

"Hey Shim (short for Shimon i.e. Simon), what do you think the Father would do to those people in Jerusalem if they tried to crucify the Master?"

"I don't know, but if I was he, I know what I'd do! I sure wouldn't want to be in their sandals."

"Me neither. I wonder what it would take to provoke those people down there into trying? Wouldn't that be interesting?"

"Why? Do you have something in mind?"

"Oh, nothing,.....just thinking."

Chapter 5

(Days 5 and 6)

Travel days #5 and #6 were no longer south, but rather almost due east down the Wadi Fari'h through the desolate Samaritan wilderness in the direction of the Jordan. The good news was that it was at least all downhill. Their next goal was the Roman fortress of Alexandrium[11] on the Jordan River *(See map on page 3)*. Although this portion of their road was noted for its robbers, no self-respecting highwayman would be so stupid as to attempt to hold up such a large group of rough-looking individuals, all carrying heavy walking sticks, chosen to be useful as cudgels. Besides, they hardly looked well-to-do. The best a robber might hope for was to sneak in at night and steal one of the group's three scrawny donkeys.

Off and on, through much of the two weary days of hiking, Judas and Levi when not too weary or during their hourly rest breaks, debated what different plans the Father, the Master, and the Sanhedrin might have for each other. Generally, such conversations would go something like:

---

[11] Alexandrium was one of nine fortresses built by Herod the Great to hold back invaders. Among these were Fortress Antonia adjacent to the Temple in Jerusalem, Masada on the Dead Sea, and Machaerus where John the Baptist was beheaded

"Levi, I'm confused. The Master has repeatedly told us he will reign over his kingdom and we as well. Fine so far. But he seems to keep telling us he'll be killed over the next few weeks! So, tell me this. If he's dead, how does he end up sitting on a throne ruling this kingdom? And then there's the minor detail of us twelve idiots who believe him? Do we end up dead too?"

"Hey man, don't ask me. I have no idea. All I know is that Jesus knows what he's doing and doesn't make mistakes. Maybe we are all to be raised from the dead too, although, I for one don't look forward to such a process.....in particular the dying first part."

Judas went on,

"And another illogical thing. If the Master knows he'll be killed by those slimy traitorous sycophants down there, then why the hell is he going? What prophet in his right mind wants to end up martyred?"

"As I remember as a boy reading the Tanakh[12], wasn't Isaiah sawn in half, and Jeremiah stoned?"

"I thought they threw Jeremiah down a well.....whatever. That sort of thing apparently happened to a lot of them. It certainly isn't an occupation with a very long life-expectancy!"

"And what about the loving Father? If he's really Jesus' father, do you mean to tell me he'd allow a slimy, weaselly little bunch of rodents like the Sanhedrin to torture his only son? ***No way man!****"*

---

[12] Jewish bible

"And what about the Master himself....his powers? We saw him appear to bring that Jairus fellow's little daughter back to life. And then there's that Centurion who claimed his servant was dead. If the Master can do that, how can a measly priest or runt of a legionnaire do anything to him?"

"Well yeah, but remember, we're not talking here about just one or two soldiers. There's a whole bloody cohort[13] *of them lodged permanently up in Fortress Antonia on the Temple Mount!"*

On and off that whole day, they kept rehashing these and similar conflicting ideas. In between, they spent their time either breathing or talking about what a good meal would be like.

That evening, they camped beneath the massive grey limestone walls of Fortress Alexandrium in the pleasant warm moist air of the Jordan Valley. Though occupied by the hated Romans, the fort did on the other hand offer security from marauders. There was already a smaller company of travelers encamped nearby. This party was on its way to the Passover as well. It had come directly down the Jordan from Tiberius to avoid having to go through Samaria. Big Jim visited their campsite. When they heard that the famous miracle worker Jesus was there, they all came over to get to see him. Their leader told Big Jim that they would be leaving at the first crack of dawn in order to reach

[13] Five hundred or so men equivalent to a U.S. Marine battalion

Jericho in one day, thereby avoiding another night worrying about bloody bandits.

Since it was near the end of the rainy season, there was still ample fresh water for them flowing down the wadi. Thus it was, that when setting up camp that first night beside the wadi, several of them couldn't help but hear Big Jim's mother giving orders,

"You two, give me your underclothing to wash while we still have water. You haven't changed in weeks and your clothes are absolutely disgusting. I'll not have you showing up in Jericho with people saying, 'What kind of a mother do those two have that would let them go around looking like that?'"

John Boy tried to respond.

"Mom it's only been a...."

"Never mind momming me young man, just give me your clothes."

Big Jim stupidly tried to intervene on his brother's behalf.

"Look here Mom there'll be plenty of water in the Jordan for......"

"And that goes for you too. Off with those clothes before I have to take them off myself."

"But...."

"Never mind the buts....the clothes!"

Philip and the others were enjoying watching the Master's pets taking it from a little woman. Not long afterward he and Nathaniel sat watching Salome down on her knees on the rough gravel at the water's edge, working like a slave pounding away at her sons' underthings.

"Nate, do you know why Jewish mothers make such great prison guards?"

"No, I'll bite, why?"

"Because they never let anyone finish a sentence!"

Before Nate could say he didn't get it, *'the Magdalene'* walked past them lugging on her shoulder a heavy pottery jug of water for cooking the evening stew. She gave them a friendly smile. Nathaniel watched as she walked away, fascinated by the swaying of her hips beneath her robe. Philip grinned.

"Now, there'll be none of that Nate my lad. You know what the boss thinks about that sort of stuff."

"Yeah yeah, I know, I know. Just because he can resist temptation, except when he loses his temper, doesn't mean I can. I just can't seem to turn off my damn imagination, no matter how hard I try. I never seem to get any better. I don't know about you Phil, but mother nature didn't make me a bloody eunuch."

"Oh, I know all right. I may be stupid, but I'm sure as hell not blind. Oh! and another thing, a little bit of free advice. Whatever you do, ***never ever*** *say anything negative concerning the Master within her hearing. Man, she'll light into you like a lioness protecting her cub! If you don't believe me, just ask 'our Leader'. Last week, I saw her tear that poor*

bastard a new one! He probably still has ringing in his ears."

They both chuckled enjoying the thought.

"Small wonder that Simon seems not to like her very much. Maybe she reminds him of his mother-in-law. So, how old do you think she is?"

"Simon's mother-in-law?"

"No asshole, 'the Magdalene'?"

"Good grief, there you go again! Anyway, I'd guess like eighteen or thereabout. And talking about tough women, if you think 'the Magdalene' is tough, just think of sweet motherly Joana. Get this. Herod hates and wants to kill this Jesus prophet right? What happens if Herod finds out that he himself is the one financing this troublemaker whose causing him more problems than 'the Baptist' did? You see, he pays Chuza to run his palace, right? Then when Chuza's not looking, his supposedly submissive, helpless little wife Joana, steals Herod's money and not only gives it to this same Jesus, but also does his wash and cooking to boot! Can you imagine how that poor browbeaten husband of hers must sweat arrowheads at night worrying about what his master would do if he ever found out? Remember, Chuza was probably the waiter the night at Machaerus[14] when they served our Master's cousin's head on a platter!"

---

[14] Herod's fortress down on the Dead sea

"Speaking of mothers-in-law, where's Simon's wife? How come she doesn't come on any of these little junkets of ours?"

"She died the year before Simon met the Lord..... probably from arguing all the time with that sweet, meek husband of hers. She was only like maybe nineteen or twenty."

"Oh, was she bossy? More importantly, was she pretty?"

"I thought she was nice looking. As to being docile and submissive, Nate my naïve lad, not long after the honeymoon, all Jewish wives are bossy and take over. I didn't know her that well. However, from what little I saw, (he chuckled at the thought) it was clear who wore the pants in the family..... and 'our leader' didn't like it. If she were still alive, I'll bet both would look forward to these trips of ours where each would have a little peace....the longer and more frequent the trip the better. John Boy on the other hand, loved her. She was always baking him sweets and treating him like her kid brother."

"I still like watching the Magdalene. I'll bet the Master does too."

"You're an idiot."

Chapter 6

(Jericho)

It was a hefty full day's march from Alexandrium to Jericho, but the road was level, and the Jordan's cool moist air on their parched skin was refreshing, as was the pleasant change from desolate rocks and sand, to the lush vegetation along the riverbanks.

Jericho was an especially interesting city for Nathaniel's first visit for several reasons. Firstly, it was probably the oldest still inhabited city in his people's history, going far back well before the time of Joseph, Moses and the others. Secondly, the air there seemed easier to breathe[15]. Thirdly, all the rich muckety-mucks from Jerusalem and Caesarea had their beautiful winter villas down there. Herod the Great had his magnificent palace with its baths and gardens, and he even built the nearby Fortress Cyprus *(named after his mother)* to protect the place. Lastly and best of all, Jericho had the finest profusion of melons, figs, dates, cucumbers, and other eatables in all Palestine.

Apparently, the small party that preceded them had alerted the city as to the coming of the now celebrated prophet Jesus from Galilee. An enthusiastic crowd was already out in the road anticipating his arrival. As they approached the outskirts of the city,

---

[15] At 850 feet below sea level, Jericho is the lowest city on earth as well as arguably of the oldest still inhabited.

Jesus noticed a little man precariously perched up in a sycamore tree beside the road.

"Who's that fellow up there?" he inquired of a bystander. The man laughed.

"He's the richest guy in town, our own one and only thieving Publican. The weasel's name is Zacchaeus. He's universally disliked. The ugly little runt climbed that tree to get a better look at you."

Jesus called up at him,

"Hey up there, you in the tree, Zacchaeus! *Come on down. I'd like to have supper at your house tonight."*

The little guy was so surprised and delighted that in clambering down, he lost his balance and ended up for a moment hanging upside down from a branch. In the process, his robe, tunic and loincloth all fell **'up'** around his chest leaving his short hairy bowlegs and more importantly his plumbing exposed for all the world to admire. The crowd as well as Jesus, burst out laughing. Once back on *terra firma*, Zacchaeus bowed and courteously invited the company to follow him to his home.

That night to all their enjoyment, Zacchaeus treated them to a banquet which included not only having their feet washed by a servant, but more importantly **meat**....a calf to be exact, wine that hadn't been watered down nor was sour, and wheat bread.....none of that cheap barely stuff. Instead of a couple figs or dates or a handful of grapes, dessert was honey cakes and melon. The meal was delicious. Even the women off eating in a separate room, for a change, enjoyed being free of cooking and being themselves waited on. It was a real treat. Zacchaeus who had no real friends, was equally pleased to show off his beautiful but melancholy home to congenial, interesting guests especially Jesus. As they reclined at dinner Jesus went to work on him,

"So Zaccheaus, tell me about yourself."

Before he knew it, the cheerless little man was telling of his lonely, unhappy life. With little subliminal directions from his guest, they were soon discussing his source of unhappiness, as well as the unhappiness he brought on the people he dealt with. Like all Jews, he was brought up knowing what Yahweh wanted. And as with many, the fog of the trials and tribulations of life obscured Yahweh. Not surprisingly, by the end of the meal,, the fog had lifted, and Jesus had another follower.

By bedtime, Judas, Levi, Nathaniel, Philip, Little Jim, and his brothers found themselves out in the courtyard. There hadn't been enough floor space or sleeping mats in Zacchaeus' house for all of them. As a result, they were out in the yard. It wasn't so much the idea of sleeping out that miffed them. After all, the weather in Jericho was pleasant....even fragrant. It was that they perceived themselves as being treated as lesser members of the Master's entourage. Levi commented,

"Well, look at it this way guys, it could be worse. Old Sour-Puss could be out here with us."

"Amen." .....from an unknown voice.

As they lay about in the dark curled up using their robes as blankets, they discussed the banquet. Judas was the one who got them off on the subject of Jesus.

"I've been thinking about how much tonight's supper cost. It must've been an arm and a leg! Why do you think this crooked tax collector did it? ....and did any of you hear that nonsense he promised Jesus while they were eating?"

One of Little Jim's brothers in the dark, probably Shim, responded,

"I did. Our generous host promised to give half his possessions to the poor.... ***half mind you!*** *Not only that, he basically said he'd stop cheating everybody. Do any of you for one second really believe that crap?"*

"Why not? Having been a Publican myself (Levi's voice), *I normally would agree with you. But then look at what happened to me! What the heck is it about the Master that almost as soon as we met him, each of us was willing to give up his career and everything to join this weird bunch? Why would any normal rational seemingly sane person do such a stupid thing?.... just up and leave everything to follow some smooth-talking rabbi? It's not that we're a lot of impressionable idealistic teenagers. Just think. At one time or another, we've all heard rabbis spout much the same sort of*

pious, idealistic stuff. Heck, just listen to the Pharisees. Certainly, none of us would have ever even considered quitting our jobs and homes to follow any of them....certainly not me. But then the Master shows up and we chuck everything to follow him. Heck, we hardly knew him, at least I didn't. Why? It's like he cast some sort of spell over us? It doesn't make sense."

Thaddeus who rarely opened his mouth contributed a thought.

"Back when I was eighteen, I had a crush on this girl. She wasn't prettier than other girls I had met, yet almost before I knew it I was head over heels in love with her. For weeks, I could think of no one else in the world. If she had encouraged me in any way, I would've followed her around like a puppy. It was love at first sight, at least for me. I think we all fell in love with Jesu somehow like that. Not sexual love mind you, but the love one feels towards the most wonderful, kind, gentle, honest, good-humored, uncompromising person we'd ever met."

A barking sound came out of the dark, probably Philip,

*"**Aarrff, Aarrff!** I don't know about you guys, but I'm moving further away from our cute pal Thaddeus here."*

(chuckling from various points of the compass)

Judas yawned and added

"You can laugh all you want, but I think it is love, love for the finest human I've ever met.....and that also goes for the man's mother."

Little Jim chimed in,

"When I was maybe ten or eleven, this traveling rabbi came to our town and spoke at the synagogue. Remember Shim? He had been everywhere: Rome, Egypt, Cyrenaic, even Babylon. He described the Pyramids, the Hanging Gardens, the Colossus of Rhodes, elephants, sea monsters, gladiator battles, you name it and he had seen it. By the end of his talk, I was ready to run away from home and follow him. Maybe the Master is in some way like that?"

"But we weren't ten years old. Hey Judas what say you to that idea?"...but all they heard coming from the hay in a far corner of the courtyard were soft ***"ZZZzzzzzzs"***. Soon the rest were doing the same. It had been a long but in the end, satisfying day.

****

Well after dawn the next morning, their *'Leader'* finally succeeded in rousing up all the contented sleepers. The distance to Zion was a good eighteen miles. It would be a long trek and every step of it uphill, a steep five-thousand-foot climb. By the time the donkeys were loaded and they were finally underway, the sun had climbed well above the Moab Mountains across the Jordan to the east. Another crowd had already gathered to get to see the famous miracle worker from Galilee. These were probably the townsfolks who had missed getting a glimpse of him the previous afternoon. On the verge of the road was a ragged emaciated blind man hoping the stories he had heard about miraculous cures were true. Most of the poorer inhabitants of Jericho were familiar with him. His name was Bartimaeus and for years now, he had been sitting at this same spot on the Jerusalem road, begging for alms. As the party was passing by, he began crying out at the top of his lungs,

"Jesus, Son of David, have mercy on me! Lord have pity on me please!"

Simon figured they'd never get out of town if the Master stopped for every person in Jericho who thought they were coming down with a cold or had a headache, so he growled down at the poor beggar.

*"**Shut up down there!** He doesn't have time for you today, maybe next time eh? We need to get to Jerusalem. So be a good fellow and knock off your yelling."*

Bartimaeus only yelled the louder,

"Son of David, have mercy on me!"

Jesus hearing the exchange, gave Simon a hard, sharp look and just said one word, "***Peter!***" Simon simply sighed and gave up. He gruffly ordered,

"OK you. Up on your feet and go on over. He wants to talk to you."

Bartimaeus sprang up and tapped his way in the direction of the sound of the other gentler voice.

Jesus spoke to the man in a kindly voice.

"Good morning. What's your name?"

"I'm Elon, son of Timaeus, but everyone just calls me Bartimaeus."

"So, Elon, what would you like from me?"

"Please Lord, I don't know what's it like to see? I've never seen the sky or a cloud."

Jesus looked into those milky white sightless eyes saying,

"Elon, do you honestly believe I can give you sight?"

"Oh yes Lord, if you ask the Father."

Jesus thought, *"Good grief, if only my guys had this much faith."*

Judas and Levi watched fascinated as the Master after laying his hands on that verminy scalp, gently ran his thumbs over those useless orbs. Suddenly Bartimaeus' jaw gapped open as he first stared down in the direction of his hands, then up at the blue sky, then everywhere at once. In a sobbing heart-rending cry, he called out to the world

"Oh God! I can see! I can see! I can see!

….and threw himself down at Jesus's ankles, sobbing uncontrollably.

"Oh thank you Rabbi, thank you."

"You're welcome Elon son of Timaeus."

With that, Simon at last had them moving again. Judas said to his companion,

"Was there ever a more amazing, wonderful human?"

"I can't imagine one except maybe for Moses and Elijah. Did you see the look on his mother's face?"

"Did you see the look on Tom's face?"

A couple of miles out of town, well after the crowd had dissipated, Simon happened to look back, and there was Bartimaeus in his rags following them with a big smile on his dirty unkempt face. Simon grumbled to himself,

"Damn! Another mouth to feed!"

Chapter 7

(Day #8 Bethany and the Holy City)

The hike that day was by far the most exhausting of the entire trip from Galilee. Almost 5,000 feet up! Not far out of Jericho they passed the Fortress of Cyprus before entering the Wadi Qelt and the most desolate, barren country of all, 'the wilderness'.

(the road up Wadi Qelt)

For the first five miles, the road clung to the wadi's north wall, rising over a thousand feet. This ascent was called the *Adummim (meaning Ascent of Blood)*. The grueling nature of the hike had put an end to all unnecessary chatter. They took their first break at an inn at the top of the Ascent. Lying resting out of the blazing sun in the shade cast by the inn, Levi started up a conversation, speaking to no one in particular. He was resting in the company of Judas, Little Simon, and the good-natured youngsters Nathaniel and Philip.

"I wonder what's going to happen when we get up to Jerusalem, what with that rumor about executing Jesus and all?"

(Judas): *"If the Sanhedrin think they are going to get away with that, they're making a big mistake. He's liable to wipe them out in a puff of smoke."*

(Shim): *"Well if he doesn't, what'll happen to us?"*

Nathaniel changed to a less disturbing subject.

"Judas, I've never been to the Holy City. What's it like?..... exciting?"

(Judas) *"I'll say. Except for Rome and maybe Alexandria, ours is the biggest in the world, especially at Passover. It's God's own holy city you know, the only one on earth. You'll see people from everywhere: and hear fifty languages. If you have the money, you can buy anything there. Caravans come through there from Africa, Egypt, Syria, and Persia. Sadly, the traitorous Sanhedrin runs it for those damned Roman bastards! But to answer your question Nate, yes, it's certainly exciting."*

(Philip): *"And now, especially exciting for us twelve.....kinda like how excited we'd be out in the desert being chased by a hungry lion!"*

(Nathaniel): "Where do you think we'll stay?"

(Judas): *"Jesus has a good friend Lazarus, who lives with his sisters in Bethany. That's just this side of the city. It's where we stayed last year. I expect it'll be the same this time. He likes stopping at friends wherever he goes. For example, from now on whenever he passes through Jericho he'll no doubt hang out with Zacchaeus.....and besides it helps to keep us from running out of funds. Speaking of funds, in the city, we'll need every shekel we have for food. It costs an arm and a leg if purchased inside the walls. Remind me to tell the ladies to do as much of their shopping as possible with the farmers outside the city."*

(Levi): "Nate, when Judas here says ***'we stayed'****, don't get your hopes up for sleeping indoors. It'll be like Zacchaeus' house last night all over again,*

(Nathaniel): *"That'll be OK so long as the weather's nice.* ***Uh-oh****, 'our leader' waving for us to get a move on. Damn, I hope the rest of the way isn't as bad as the last five hours were."*

As they got up groaning, Levi inquired,

"Phil, do ya think this is the inn the Master was referring to in his story about the 'Good Samaritan'?"

"Probably. This is the most notorious bandit country in all Palestine. The last time we passed this way, I noticed him talking to the innkeeper. That's most likely where the idea came from."

When he saw the look of concern on his walking companion's face, he laughed.

"Don't worry my law-abiding Publican. If anyone tangles with Simon, Jim and Andy they'll regret it."

"Really?"

"Yeah, really. Those three gentlemen have gotten into more than one brawl with the other fishermen on the lake trying to steal their catch or horn in on their spot. Haven't you noticed their walking sticks? They are about twice as heavy as yours. If they were any heavier, they'd be war clubs."....and he laughed adding, *".....and have you noticed the long knife Simon carries? It's practically a sword! Believe me, those guys are no bloody angels."*

"I wonder why the Master picked them?"

"Why did he pick you?"

"Good point."

So much for worrying about highwaymen!

It was almost dusk when they arrived at the tiny hamlet of Bethany. It was on a hillside about two miles from the city and consisted of no more than a couple dozen dwellings many of them poor, one or two-room, clay floored, mud-brick affairs, with wattle roofs covered with clay. These, along with a stone well and a small stone synagogue made up the village. More important, was the magnificent view afforded one looking down on the City of David and the beautiful Temple Herod the Great built.

Jesus was welcomed by a pale-looking young man named Lazarus along with his kid sister Mary and his older sister Martha. Nathaniel murmured to his sidekick,

"Damnit Phil, don't people in this country ever name their girls anything but Mary? I can barely keep track of ours as is.....except for 'the Magdalene'. What was that woman like around here a generation ago that everyone named their daughter after? She must've been something else."

"Whoever she was, she also must've been nice if she was anything like our flock of Marys."

Lazarus and his sisters were well off and had a nice well-kept home made of stone with a real tile roof. But it wasn't nearly large enough to house all of them which now also included Bartimaeus who after being given his sight refused to be driven off by Simon. So, more or less the same group of 'second class citizens' *(now including Bartimaeus)* ended up sleeping out on the grassy slope of the Mount of Olives. It was a beautiful, clear, cool night with millions of bright stars for their canopy. As they lay there, Bartimaeus exclaimed,

"Oh my!"

Nathan who was lying next to the ragged but happy beggar whispered,

"What is it Elon?"

"The heavens! I've never seen stars before. They are so beautiful. What a good job God did on them, don't you think?"

"I never thought of that Elon, I just took it for granted. Thanks for reminding me. I meant to ask you earlier, what was it like, ya know, having the Master cure you?"

"I'll never forget it. I was sitting there by the side of the road with my begging bowl like always. It was already hot and I was as usual hungry. Then I heard a lot of voices approaching. I asked "Hey! someone please tell me what's going on?" A voice said, "It's Jesus that miracle worker from Galilee, he's heading this way." So I began shouting to this Jesus, and a rude voice told me "Shut up!"...but I kept shouting all the louder. What the hell, what else had I to lose?....nothing. Then this wonderful, gentle voice told me to come over. I got up and felt my way towards the voice. It kindly asked me my name, and what I wanted. So, I naturally told it that I wanted to see. The next thing I knew he was gently touching my worthless flat eyes, and suddenly there was a burst of light, ***and there he was!*** *The first thing I ever saw in my wretched life was Jesus. Just as suddenly I wasn't miserable or depressed or bitter anymore. For the first time in my*

memory, I felt at peace and was happy. You can't believe how wonderful it was."

"I'm happy for you Elon, and glad you are with us."

"Thanks Nate..... thanks."

Different voices in the dark:

"What time do you think it is?"

"Too early to go to sleep, maybe the second hour (8 pm). Phil, tell us a story."

"No please, anything but that (probably Levi). *Nate start a song that we all know, and we'll join in."*

(Nate)*:" I wish someone had a lyre. I wonder if 'the Magdalene' plays?"*

"Nate, for heaven's sake, will you forget her and just sing."

Nathaniel's tenor voice began the familiar song and one by one they all joined in, even Elon:

♫ How beautiful you are, my darling! Oh, how beautiful!

♪ Your eyes behind your veil are doves. Your hair is like a flock of goats descending from the hills of Gilead.

♫ Your lips are like a scarlet ribbon;

Your temples behind your veil are like the halves of a pomegranate.

♪Your breasts are like two fawns, like twin fawns of a gazelle that browse among the lilies.

After that, it was one song after another, mostly from Solomon, and most bringing back memories of girls they had once loved. By the third hour, they began drifting off to sleep until the only sound was that of the warm evening breeze coming up from the south.

****

Levi was the first to wake the next morning, probably because he was more used to sleeping indoors, and being older, his bones and muscles were more susceptible to sleeping on cold, hard earth with nothing but his robe for a blanket. The sun had just begun peeping over the desolate hills and dry wadis to the east, and its rays were reflecting off the walls of the city below.

"Hey you guys, quick. Wake up. Look at the city and Temple. Quick, rise and shine, don't miss this!"

Nathaniel was the last to sit up, and there below him was his first real view of the *City of David!* In Bartimaeus' case, it was even more breathtaking. Remember, he had never seen sky, stars, wadis, inns, people, or water before, **and now Jerusalem!** By the sun's early light, the walls of the city appeared pinkish. To their right, at the northeastern quarter of the city rose the vast, gleaming, cream-colored limestone Temple area. At the northern end of the Temple precinct loomed ominous, gray Fortress Antonia where a Roman cohort was permanently garrisoned, ready to quell any riot with their swords and lances *(see page 67)*. At the southeastern corner of the Temple area, the height from the top of the corner tower to the floor of the Kidron Valley was a straight drop of well over sixty feet. Levi explained to Nate and Elon that this corner was referred to as the *'pinnacle of the Temple'*. He then pointed out across the far side of the city, the *Upper City or Mount Zion* containing Herod's palace with its fortified towers. That was where the priests and upper-class lived.

After a breakfast of bread, cheese and melon, Judas who knew the city best having lived there, led them all the two miles downhill, across the Kidron Valley, then up through the Golden Gate onto the Temple Mount. The Temple Mount was a massive thirty-acre rectangular courtyard. Its periphery consisted of tall, magnificent marble colonnades, while in the center was the glittering golden Temple with its many courts. Philip acted as tour guide for awed Nathaniel and Bartimaeus.

"The entire area surrounding the Temple is called the 'Courtyard of the Gentiles'. Look over there Elon and read what that sign says."

"I don't know how to read."

"Oh, sorry, I forgot. Here, you Nate tell us what it says."

"Some of it looks like Latin and Greek which I can't read either Elon, so don't feel too bad. But the Hebrew is a warning that any gentile found within the Temple itself will be stoned."

While that was going on, Jesus had entered the Temple through the main entrance called '*the Beautiful Gate*'. The first inner courtyard was called the *Courtyard of Women.* Philip explained to his companions that this was as far as a Jewish woman was allowed to proceed. Here and there, public speakers were arguing vociferously, debating before clusters of onlookers about religious and political issues. He explained that this is where the Master would probably spend most of the week teaching. The next courtyard in, was the *Courtyard of the Israelites (men)*. After that, came the *Courtyard of the Priests* where the Temple altar for sacrificing animals and burnt offerings was located.

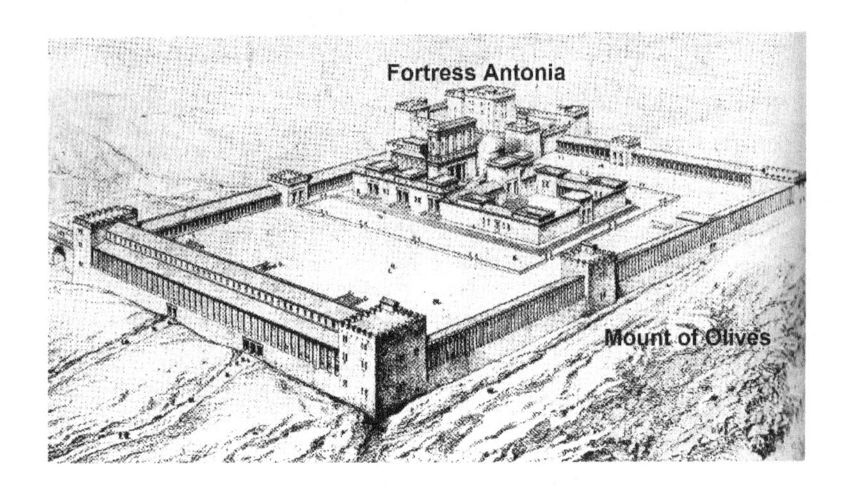

Nathaniel interrupted his unpaid tour guide.

"And where is the 'Holy of Holies'?"

"It's the innermost chamber, now just an empty dark room which was where the Ark would be kept had it not mysteriously disappeared at the time the Babylonians destroyed Solomon's Temple."

"What do you think happened to the Ark?"

"Jerimiah and the Maccabees say it was hidden in a wadi cave a few miles east of here and the entrance covered up. Someday someone will stumble across it. Won't that be a day for us Jews!"

Nathaniel and Elon stood like a couple of country bumpkins watching the heterogeneous crowd milling about and seeing smoke rising from sacrifices further in. Philip explained that here was where Jesus spent most of his time last year, teaching, and arguing with the Pharisees. Then in the evenings, he would usually go down to a garden at the base of the Mount of Olives for some quiet time of prayer and meditation.

****

That evening they had another good feed, this time with chicken. That meant they had meat again, twice in three days! The meal wasn't nearly as sumptuous as Zacchaeus', but as Thomas commented afterward to Judas,

"It sure beats the hell out of lentil stew!"

That night lying out on the hillside in his robe, Judas began chuckling. Levi was puzzled.

"What?"

"I was watching the Master while Lazarus' sisters served us tonight. He never said a word to Martha. And did you notice how hard kid sister Mary was working?" *(Judas was chuckling again)*

"So?" this time from Philip.

"Remember what happened last year between the Master and Martha?"

At that all of them lying about began to chuckle, that is except for Nathaniel and Bartimaeus. Both newcomers were curious, especially Nathaniel.

"What happened last year that was so funny?"

"The Master met his match, that's what."

"You're kidding right? That's hard to believe. Who? Tell us."

Philip interrupted, *"Here, let me tell the story."*

(Levi): *"Is there any way we can ever stop you?"*

Philip grinned and began.

"Last year when we visited here, Lazarus' kid sister Mary fell in love with the Master. He was her hero. She would sit at his feet the entire day listening to his stories and little homilies. In the meantime, big sister was busting her ass sweeping the tile floors, making sure nothing was left unfolded or slightly out of place, kneading and baking the day's bread, shopping, and on this day after all of that, preparing a big supper. Finally, she couldn't take it any longer and went to where we all were talking. She just stood there with her hands on her hips glaring down at Mary.

"Well?" *she said, "Are you going to help or am I going to have to do everything by myself!?"*

The Master saw that she was pissed off, and in his familiar gentle way began schmoozing her.

"Now Martha, dear Martha, don't let little unimportant thing upset you."

He went on like this, with her listening stone-faced to her celebrated guest. Then he made a mistake. The Master doesn't make many mistakes, but he did that day. He was messing with the wrong woman. He said something like,

"Martha sweetheart, your house cleaning, doing the wash, cooking, and all that sort of women's work is not really what's important. What Mary is doing listening to me on the other hand is."

He didn't get to continue because Martha simply spun on her heel and went back to her cooking. The Master must've figured out that he had once again succeeded in 'calming the troubled waters' as was his way....but he hadn't. We all found that out the next evening when we returned from a day at the Temple famished.... ***and there was no food! Nothing!*** *No bread had been baked and nothing was cooking in the courtyard. Mary and her brother were horrified! (failure to furnish hospitality in the Middle East was considered an insult). About then Martha showed up. Mary just gasped,*

"Martha, where's supper? Where's the bread?"

"Oh, did no one remember to take care of that today? Well don't let it worry you, it's not important. I myself spent the day praying and meditating as every ***woman*** *should. Right Rabbi?"*

And with that, she smiled at Jesus and walked out of the room. The Master wisely never said a word. For supper that night we all had ***'skip'*** *to eat, other than a few grapes some of us found still left on the vines in the garden. The next morning there was still no food of course. I watched as we were all leaving. Mary had started to go with us, but paused at the door and glanced over at her sister who was just standing there. Martha smiled and said,*

"Have a nice day with Jesus today. I think I might visit the Temple again....you know, to pray."

Poor Mary burst into tears and turned back into the house. That evening we had an especially good feed. But I noticed Mary's eyes were red. I also noticed that at supper the Master kept his mouth shut, never uttering a word. He had made a mistake, and he knew it. That was one woman he didn't plan to tangle with again!"

****

The most humorous event that week at the Temple was the incident of the blind beggar with chutzpah[16]. That evening, John Boy narrated the story to Martha and Mary who had stayed home to nurse her brother who wasn't feeling well.....**and to cook!**

"*There was this middle-aged scrawny beggar blind from birth. Apparently, he had sat daily for years begging on the steps of the Beautiful Gate, where all of the Temple priests, Levites[17], and Temple guards knew him. His name is Aryeh. Anyway, yesterday morning our Master stopped to chat with the poor guy. Next thing we knew after laying his hands on the man's head, he mixed some spit and dirt and put it on the guy's eyes. He then told him to go wash them off at the Pool of Siloam[18] (see page 4). The poor guy must've believed the Master, otherwise, he would've assumed it*

[16] supreme self-confidence, nerve, gall
[17] Money changers and custodians of the Temple
[18] A pool at the very southeast corner of the city by the Tekoa Gate

to be a nasty prank played on a helpless blind man and not blindly stumbled all the way down to the far corner of the city to the pool. So, as he later told the Master, he went and washed, and lo and behold, like our new friend Bartimaeus here, **he too could see!** *Naturally, he went running and leaping all over town like a demented newborn gazelle, shouting to everyone what this kind voice with a Galilean accent had done. Of course, our beloved High Priest heard about it and knew damn well who this stranger with the accent was. So, his angry Lordship had the happy fellow's poor parents dragged in to be questioned. Had their son really been born blind he demanded, or was this some sort of beggar's scam? Well, the parents weren't born yesterday. They knew as did everyone in the city, that it's never a good idea to piss off the High Priest. So, this Jewish mother's evasive reply must've been something like,*

"Look, you intelligent gentlemen of the Sanhedrin have all been observing this blind man day in and day out for years and therefore must know more about such things than uneducated people like us."

Then she weaseled out by noting that their son was of age and could best answer for himself.

So, they had the ecstatic fellow man brought in and rudely asked if he really had been blind.

"Have you gentlemen been entering the Temple all these years and never noticed me with my useless milky eyes begging? Everyone else has. Did you never

even look into my face or eyes,,,,, eyes that could barely distinguish day from night?"

Ignoring his embarrassing question one of them ordered.

"If you can really see now, then read what I just wrote down on this slate."

"I can't."

"Aa Haa! So you can't see!"

***"I said I can't read, not that I can't see!** I assumed it would be obvious to learned gentlemen like yourselves that I couldn't possibly have learned to read, having been blind from birth up until a few hours ago! But if any one of you would hold up an object, I'll gladly describe it."*

The interrogation clearly wasn't improving the High Priest's disposition any, so he changed the line of questioning.

"How did this strange man cure you? Was it by Beelzebub?

Now Aryeh like his parents, wasn't a dummy.

*"Look. All I know is that until a few hours ago I was totally blind. Then this stranger comes to me, rubs my eyes, prays to Yahweh not Beelzebub, tells me to wash in Siloam, and now I can see, How all this happened, I haven't the foggiest idea. Isn't that what scholars like you should explain? Certainly not some poor ignorant ex-blind man **who can't even read!"***

But the smart assed fellow just couldn't resist poking the High Priest in the eye one last time. He innocently inquired,

"So, am I to take it then, that you gentlemen believe Beelzebub goes around doing good deeds like curing blind men?"

By now the High Priest was so angry and frustrated, that he ordered the Temple Guards to kick Aryeh out with a stern warning not to go around repeating this ***'nonsense'*** *about having been cured.*

*Poor Caiaphas who now felt with some justification that he had made a fool of himself, began venting his spleen on the Temple guards, shouting at them to henceforth arrest Jesus for the slightest infraction of Temple rules, "****...anything! You hear me!?....Anything!****"*

In the meantime, Aryeh went back and found the Master, telling him everything that happened. The Master laughed so hard at the way the happy guy told the story, that he had tears in his eyes,

****

By now, the Sanhedrin and Pharisees were more determined than ever to curb this Galilean troublemaker. Each day their confrontations with him grew more frequent and intense, and would usually end up with them angrily retreating with their tails between their legs. Jesus advised the crowd who witnessed these confrontations,

"Practice our religion the way these rabbis tell you, but not the way they do. They don't practice what they preach. Everything these hypocrites do is for show. These teachers of the law, pretend to be holy on the outside but on the inside are like everyone else, even worse!"

He finally provoked them too far. So, when they began picking up stones, he realized now was a good time to make himself scarce and retreat. That night, he decided to go back to Jericho and across the Jordan for a little peace and quiet.

Chapter 8

(Lasarus)

The next morning, they departed Bethany early to avoid attracting a crowd. It was a gorgeous day without a cloud in the sky. They all thanked Martha and Mary and hoped Lazarus would feel better from whatever it was he had. Martha the ever-gracious hostess, was nonetheless happy to see them off. A week was a long time to have guests especially that many. Her view which she was careful to keep to herself, was that *after three days, fish and visitors both begin to smell.*

The trip this time was *'a piece of cake',* all downhill. As usual, there was little chit-chat when on these long thirsty treks. What was said, was always light; never controversial. Their energy went into hiking, not talking or bickering. However, that didn't mean they didn't think. Judas for example, pondered over why Jesus was leaving the city? With his great powers, how could he possibly be afraid of the Pharisees? Judas for one, was confused, but then again, not a few things Jesus said and did confused them.

By noon they had reached the inn where they were able to drink as much water as they wanted and refill their water skins. By late afternoon, Jesus who somehow never understood the concept of overstaying one's welcome, stopped at Zacchaeus' house.

After supper as before, the lesser cliques retreated out to the stable where they curled up in their robes on the straw. Though tired from the day's march and it was dark, it was still too early to sleep, so they critiqued recent events.....Lazarus....the hike....the smart-assed blind guy Aryeh....the good food, etc. It was Judas who brought up the subject of the Pharisees and their increased animosity.

"What the heck is the Master up to, running out of the city like that? Are we celebrating the Passover there or what?"

Different voices chimed in out of the dark.

"Yeah, I agree. What are we doing backtracking all the way down here to Jericho? Are we now going to have to turn around and make that awful climb back up? I don't get it."

"Well, he must have a plan of some kind. He doesn't do things like trekking our asses all the way down here for no reason. I say he's got a clever plan to somehow screw the damn Pharisees."

"Knowing he doesn't make mistakes is comforting, that is if we forget about his tangling with Mistress Martha."

"Maybe he's going to take Simon's advice and go back to Galilee where it's safe."

"Don't get your hopes up."

"He said he's going to Jerusalem to be crucified right? But he can't very well become king and drive out the Romans if he's dead. Maybe he meant that they

were going to ***only try to*** *crucify him. That makes more sense. Say Phil, what does your buddy Andy say about all of this?"*

"The big boys over in the house don't know what's going on any more than we idiots out here with the other donkeys. But they all believe that we'll eventually be running the country instead of the Procurator and good King[19] *Herod's two sons, just not when."*

Mention of the hypocritical Pharisees reminded Philip of a joke.

"Do you guys know the story of the rabbi and his stolen donkey?"

"Oh no!" a voice out of the dark probably Levi, *"...but I'm sure you'll tell us anyway."*

"Correct. There once was this impoverished Pharisee, a rabbi, and someone stole his donkey. So, he went to complain to the elder Rabbi at the synagogue. You see, he wanted to get back his donkey, but didn't have the foggiest idea how. The elder suggested the way to do it, was to shame the thief into giving back the donkey.

"How do I do that?"

"Next Sabbath stand up at the readings and briefly review Moses' commandments, one at a time. Start with the first in a low, calm voice, "I am the Lord thy God .etc. etc. Then raising your voice just a bit, hit

---

[19] Herod the Great murdered, his wife, his mother-in-law, multiple sons as well as half of the Sanhedrin!

the second a lick, "Thou shalt not take the name of the Lord thy God in vain, etc. etc.". With each successive commandment raise your voice a bit louder until reaching the seventh, "Thou shalt not steal!". By then you need to be jumping up and down and shouting. Then for the remaining three commandments rapidly taper back down to your normal, calm voice level. I'll bet whoever stole your donkey will be shamed into returning it."

So, on the following Sabbath, the Pharisee began one commandment at a time, followed by a brief comment, each time raising his voice a little louder.

"I am the Lord thy God. Thou shalt not have strange gods...."

"Thou shalt not take the name of the Lord..."

"Remember to keep holy the Sabbath..."

"Honor thy father and mother..."

"Thou shalt not kill...." *(by now he was waving his arms and shouting about Cain killing Able etc.)*

"Thou shalt not commit adultery! *...(suddenly a long pause and no comment)*

"Thou shalt not Steal"
(no comments from here on).

"Thou shalt not bear false witness...."

"Thou shalt not covet thy neighbor's wife."

"Thou shalt not covet thy neighbor's goods."

After the service, the elder couldn't wait to ask why the Pharisee hadn't given the seventh commandment a pounding? The Pharisee coughed and sheepishly replied,

"You know Rabbi, when I got to the sixth commandment, I suddenly remembered where I left my donkey."

(laughter out of the dark followed by Levi's voice)

"Ya know Phil, the Master might consider that a low-class joke."

"I know. That's why I told you guys!"

(more hoots and chuckles out of the dark)

Nathaniel made matters worse saying as expected,

"I don't get it."

Soon all but Judas were all peacefully snoring away. He was lying on his back staring up. He was thinking about what one of them had just said about them **only trying to** crucify him.

The next morning, they waded across the Jordan into Peraea *(See map on page 3)*.

****

Over the succeeding couple of days, the local sick and curious soon heard that Jesus the prophet from Galilee was in the vicinity, and he taught and cured many of them. Happily, he was free from the stress of confrontations with the Pharisees. On the second day, a message arrived from Bethany. It was succinct:

Lord, please come quick. Lazarus whom you love is sick to death.

Martha

Much to the surprise of the twelve, instead of showing concern for the family that showed them so much hospitality and hastening back, Jesus continued with his curing and kept teaching. Simon mentioned it.

"Master, your good friend Lazarus is perhaps dying. Aren't you concerned? Why aren't we going back?"

"Relax Peter, I know what I'm doing."

They recrossed the Jordan early the next morning heading for Bethany. With the additional arduous miles to cover, they didn't pause in Jericho, no doubt to the relief of Zacchaeus.

It was growing dusk when a mile or so short of their destination, Jesus sent the youngsters John and Nathaniel hurrying on ahead to alert the two sisters. It therefore came as no surprise, when a few hundred yards from Bethany they saw ahead a woman slumped on a boulder by the side of the road. When she saw him approaching, she ran sobbing to meet him falling to her knees at his feet. It was Martha,

"Oh Lord, *(tears streaming down her cheeks)* ***if only you had been here! If you had been here, he'd still be alive! Oh Lord, why didn't you come?"***

Judas had been walking with the Master and Simon discussing the money situation. Both he and Simon were touched seeing tears in the Master's eyes, but they agreed with Martha. Why in the world had he waited till it was too late? It didn't seem like him, especially considering how much he loved this family.

Poor Mary was too brokenhearted to even go down the road to meet her *beau ideal*. She had been of almost no help to her sister. Thus it was Martha who had been overwhelmed with the funeral arrangements, tasked with washing and perfuming his body, combing and trimming his hair and beard, dressing him, tying his jaw shut, binding his wrists together over his stomach, and wrapping him in a white linen shroud *(there was no embalming or body wrapping as the Egyptians did)*. Within eight hours of his death, he was already safely entombed.

The burial site was a short walk away, on the slope of the Mount of Olives, a tiny cave-like affair cut out of the limestone rock. Inside were three ledges on which to lay bodies. This tomb was intended to also someday house the sisters. Once Lazarus had been laid inside, a large limestone wheel was rolled across the entrance and whitewashed to indicate that a corpse was putrefying within.

The next morning Jesus asked to be taken to the tomb. Judas and the others along with several of the neighbors tagged along never knowing what to expect next. When Jesus asked to have the tomb opened, they all heard Martha and a couple of neighbors meekly object. The sisters were upset enough without having the smell of their own brother to contend with as well. But Jesus was insistent. Andrew and Simon who were told to shoulder the stone back, certainly didn't care much for the idea,

Then it was suddenly clear to all that the Master had lost his sense of reality and gone over the edge, because he called in,

"Hey Lazarus, come on out. It's me, Jesus. I want to talk to you."

Most of them particularly Thomas, remembered back when Jesus told the Centurion that his dying servant would live. And then there was the official who said his little daughter was dead. In both those cases, the individuals might have been in some sort of coma, or as the Master put it *"sleeping"*. But this time was different. There was no *'might have been'*. Lazarus had been buried in there **for four whole days!** He wasn't sleeping or in any damned coma,,,,**he was dead!....and he wasn't going to be coming out!** No doubts this time! Here was poor Master trying to carry on a conversation with a rotting corpse! They were all embarrassed for him.....and themselves as well. They all truly loved this man, but this time he had finally gone off into his own fantasy world. In the long pregnant silence that followed, they wondered when it would finally sink in to him, that the only thing that was going to come out of that tomb was a nauseating odor. Judas felt sorry for him. He found himself wishing that they had remained back up in Galilee where they belonged. Now the Judeans would be convinced that they were nothing more than a bunch of stupid, gullible country hicks from up north led by a loony.

Suddenly there was an audible collective gasp from everyone.....a gasp of fear.....of horror!. **A shrouded bent over figure was attempting to hobble out of the low tomb entrance!**

As children, the boogeyman they were threatened with if bad, was a mummy coming after them in the dark, from out of Egypt. And here before their very eyes was that very thing!.....**coming for them!** Jesus broke the spell.

"Well? Is somebody going to help the man before he trips and breaks a leg?! Peter! Untie his hands and face and pull off that shroud."

It took a few moments of stunned inaction before Simon reluctantly advanced towards **it**. Andrew held back until his brother hissed,

*"**Andy!** If I'm going to touch **it**, so are you!"*

Once untied and freed of the shroud, a seemingly perfectly healthy, cheerful, friendly-looking Lazarus went up to Jesus, and the two of them greeted and hugged each other. But when Lazarus tried to kiss his sisters, they jumped back with a gurgled cry of fright. He simply said,

"Hey girls, it's just me. Don't be afraid."

He next smiled and greeted the others,

"Yahead shlamlak" ("Hello")

They never answered; merely stood there frozen, with their mouths agape like twelve idiots. He then asked,

"Hey what time is it? Is anybody besides me hungry? Martha, what's there to eat?"

****

This miracle did it! All lingering unadmitted doubts were gone, even with Didymus[20]. Their master was really what he had been saying all along, the historically prophesied Messiah who would defeat and drive off the Romans.

It didn't take long before the Lazarus story spread like wildfire across the city. The High Priest of course, was one of the first to hear of it. He and most of the Sanhedrin were furious at this insulting Galilean fraud's latest trick to stir up the people.

---

[20] Thomas' nickname

****

For the seventy-one members of the Sanhedrin, life until recently had been relatively pleasant and carefree....that is, so long as they did the bidding of their Roman overlords, and didn't allow trouble to be stirred up. True, the typical poor Jew was being overtaxed, but at least he wasn't being butchered. But now, in particular, since yesterday, this damned rabbi from the backwoods of Galilee was upsetting the apple cart. For the umpteenth time over the past hundred years, a rabble-rouser was succeeding in stirring up the people's foolish false hopes. The common people yearned for the Messiah who would drive out the pagan foreign oppressors. It seemed that every few years, some hothead zealot would arrive on the scene from nowhere and stir up rioting. Only a couple Passovers back, on orders from Procurator Pilate, the Cohort had stormed out of Fortress Antonia into the streets of the city putting the rioters to the sword!

The people never seemed to learn. The results were always the same: a lot of dead stupid Jews and the bloody Romans still there. Nobody was going to defeat them, least of all this country bumpkin. So why fight battles you are bound to lose? It was the height of stupidity. For the Sanhedrin, clearly something had to be done before it was too late. If only they could get rid of this latest religious nutcase, they would probably save hundreds, maybe even thousands of lives, ...and more importantly possibly their own! It was therefore decided by the majority, to find some excuse to get the Romans to put the Nazarene to death for the good of all. Better one dead Jew than hundreds. It sounded heartless but made hard perfect sense. This Jesus fellow seemed to have been going around saying how he wanted to die for the people. Well, here was his chance.....**and theirs**.

Almost immediately Jesus was made aware of this decision from one of the members of that august body who was a secret disciple. Judas also knew from one of the servants who was a Zealot mole, that they intended to arrest Jesus and have the Romans execute him. With this threat in mind, that same evening, Jesus and the others slipped out the Damascus Gate *(northern gate)* and traveled thirteen miles north to a safehouse in the village of Ephraim *(see page 3)* where they holed up till Passover Week.

****

Judas in the meanwhile was beginning to fantasize about what he and Little Simon might do. The options that his fertile mind imagined were three.

1) Do nothing at all and see what happens.
2) Go secretly to the Sanhedrin and convince them to cool things off by quietly seizing the Master and sequestering him in a jail for the duration of the Passover. Then scaring him

into returning to Galilee by threat of crucifixion.

3) Provoking them into trying to actually crucify him. Wouldn't that be something to watch and write home about? If he could so easily give life to a corpse, or give Bartimaeus and Aryeh their sight, how much easier to cause the man trying to nail him to the cross to go blind?!.....or better yet the High Priest?....or even his Imperial Majesty the Procurator? ......or simply strike them all dead and take over?! An even more appealing thought had the Father raining down fire and brimstone on all the bastards?

Just thinking about option #3 gave him more pleasure than thinking back on the girl he once was in love with. He needed to get *Shim* off to the side somewhere and discuss this. The problem was that *Shim* was one of *'them'*. All he needed was for the Master to find out what he was thinking!

Chapter 9

(Palm Sunday week)

It was the evening of the day they returned from Ephraim….the first day of Passover Week. Martha had prepared a special supper in honor of the Master in thanks for returning Lazarus to them. Jesus and his crew were reclining at table with Lazarus, enjoying honey cake for dessert. Martha and Mary had waited on them all including the other 'Marys' in the next room. The dirty dishes had just been taken away. The men were discussing the events of the day when Mary came in and knelt at the feet of her lord. She had with her a porcelain container of expensive fragrant spikenard[21] which she opened and carefully poured over Jesus' feet. She then lovingly massaged it in and wiped them with her long soft black hair. Judas who knew the price of things grumbled to Little Simon who was lying beside him.

"Good grief Shim. Here we are, almost broke, and this silly girl has gone and spent enough on that perfume to pay for our entire return trip to Galilee. She could've just as well have used olive oil or even water from the village well."

Jesus heard him and turned,

"Leave poor Mary alone Judas. She's been through a tough week and just wants to show her thanks. You worry too much about money. The Father

[21] A perfume oil made from certain flowers

will provide. Do you see the sparrows worrying about money?"

"No, Rabbi, but the sparrows don't have to eat your mother's lentil-onion stew!"

Philip got Mary to smile when he quipped,

"Mary, you at least could've saved a little of that stuff for Shim's feet. I had the misfortune of sleeping near him last night, and had to move because of his feet's pungent fragrance."

Little Simon defended himself.

"I can't help it, but at least I bathe once in a while ***Philip****."*

"Philip is it? Oh poor me! This morning it was Phil. Does that mean we aren't pals any more Shim?"

They all laughed, even Andrew who still suspected that Judas *'borrowed'* a little of the crew's money for himself from time to time. But remembering the last time he expressed such concerns within hearing of the Master, he kept his mouth shut. Jesus then looked down at the girl who had tears of devotion in her eyes.

"Martha and I love you Lord. Thank you again for giving us back our brother."

"You're welcome Mary, both of you."

****

The next morning, they headed for the city as usual. This day however things were quite different. They had barely gone a hundred yards before running into little clusters of neighborhood people who knew Lazarus. They had gathered along the roadside to see and cheer the prophet who had raised him from the tomb. Jesus stopped and signaled the two youngsters.

"John Boy and Nate, do me a favor please. Run on ahead to Bethphage[22]. The other day, I noticed a man there who has a white donkey. Ask him if I might please borrow it to ride into the city."

A worried Simon, interrupted.

"Rabbi?"

"What is it Peter?"

"Why in the world are you doing this?.....riding instead of walking? You never ride. And besides, do you think it's a good idea? Riding into the city at Passover no less. It's kinda ya know, kinda like some sort of king or a Judah Maccabeus[23] about to trigger a revolt. Why unnecessarily go out of our way to piss off the powers that be?"

"Peter, a king bent on revolution comes in riding on a charger, not a lowly donkey. A king bent on peace, rides in on a donkey. Anyway, thanks for the advice, but I know what I'm doing."

"OK, have it your own way, but don't blame me later when the police are chasing us!....and by the way, what's wrong with our donkeys?"

---

[22] A tiny hamlet a mile east of the temple, halfway between Bethany and the city

[23] 200 years earlier, Judah Maccabeus led a successful revolt reconquering all Israel.

"None are white."

John and Nathaniel jogged on ahead, and in the little hamlet, they spotted a white donkey in one of the mudbrick huts' yard. They knocked and made their request,

"Jesus, the prophet from Galilee would like to borrow your donkey if you don't mind."

"Jesus? Really? Sure. I'm not using it at the moment. Just be careful not to overload it and to get it back to me today. What's he want it for anyway?"

"To ride I suppose, but we aren't certain. Until just now, he's always walked. We'll bring it back as soon as we reach the Golden Gate. Thanks a lot."

Jesus had just started down the hill to the Kidron Valley when John and Nathaniel met him with the donkey. The two used their robes to make a sort of seat on the little animal and he mounted.

People from the city who had heard about Lazarus, and that Jesus was coming were gathering beside the road below. With Simon leading the way, they approached the excited throng. Children and dogs were running along beside him. People were yelling things like,

"Hosanna to the Son of David!" and ***"Blessed is he who comes in the name of the Lord!"*** and ***"Blessed is the king of Israel!"***

It was this latter *'king'* cheer that was later reported to the High Priest by his agents who had infiltrated the crowd. The spies estimated the crowd to be well over a thousand people, some of whom even threw palm fronds[24] out on the road ahead of the donkey.

When Jesus' entourage reached the Golden Gate on the eastern wall below the Temple, the people there wanted to know what all the commotion was about.

"It's that Jesus fellow from Galilee, you know, the prophet who raised that man from the dead. Some

[24] In the ancient Near East and Mediterranean world, the palm branch was a symbol of victory, triumph, peace, and eternal life

say he's the Messiah. Whoever he is, we hope he gives these damned Roman pigs a poke in the eye."

****

During his subsequent trips to the Temple that week to teach, crowds gathered to listen to this popular wonderworker, and in hopes of maybe witnessing a miracle. It was on his second visit, that one of the Levite money changers in the Courtyard of the Women, rudely shouted at him to move elsewhere because he was disrupting the line at his table. He was a nasty little fat guy. Now in those days one rarely saw a person in all Palestine who wasn't lean?......who had an ounce of fat on him or her? Never!.... unless he was rich, a Publican, or a priest. Well, this day was one of the rare occasions any of them ever saw the Master lose his temper. It was scary, especially in light of what he had just done with Lazarus, not to mention the lepers, blind men, and the like! With a fierce, angry look on his normally tranquil features, he turned on the loud-mouthed moneychanger[25] and overthrew his table, sending coins in every direction. He then pulled off his leather belt and as the shocked man frantically bent over to retrieve his precious money, Jesus began flailing him across his broad backside. It was a sight to see; the poor fellow running and yelling for help from

[25] The temple tax could only be paid in Phoenician shekels, no other coins were permitted, thus almost all money required changing!

the temple guards. Neither guards, nor bystanders however, felt the slightest shade of sympathy for this well-fed tax collector. Instead, they were all laughing, enjoying the spectacle.

(Courtyard of the Women where Jesus preached. Steps lead to the Courtyard of the Israelites)

****

That evening the High Priest came to a decision, He was meeting with Rubin Barlazar, the Pharisee who headed up his Special Action Committee.

"Things have gotten out of hand Rubin. Yesterday people were calling him the king, and others the Messiah. There could easily have been a riot started. Today he disrupted the routine Temple activities. What will he do tomorrow eh? The Passover is in four days, with crowds gathering in the city. It's time to act."

"I can have the Temple guards grab him first thing in the morning, as soon as he and his band of gullible fishermen arrive at the Temple. If necessary, we'll have drawn swords."

"Good grief! Don't do that! Too many people favor him. First thing you know, you'll be the one who provoked the riot. That in turn would bring out the Romans at a trot. Have you noticed this week that they've doubled the number of legionnaires patrolling in pairs around up on top of the colonnade[26], each now carrying his pilum (javelin)? The thing to do, is arrest him after dark when the people are all home in their beds, preferably in an isolated place. Get your spies to find out his evening whereabouts. But do it soon."

"One of our servants knows one of his gang of fishermen. I'll see if I can get hold of him."

---

[26] The perimeter of the Temple Mount. See page 67

"If you have to, offer him a bribe. At a time like this, a few shekels is the least of our problems."

"How far can I go?"

"Start with thirty denarii. You can go as high as fifty."

Chapter 10

(the Last Supper)

Jesus called Judas over,

"Judas, since you know it best, I want you to go into town please, and arrange for a place to celebrate our Seder[27]*. With the city full of visitors, if we don't act quickly, there may not be any decent places left. Take someone with you to give you a hand. Do you have enough money?"*

Normally the Master showed blissful unconcerned about money. It drove poor Judas crazy….and he sure didn't want another lecture about the damn birds of the air and flowers in the field not worrying about money!

"Just barely. I hate to ask for any more from Lazarus or our ladies. They've already been overly generous."

Young Nathaniel who along with Bartimaeus was nearby, spoke up.

"Can I go with you Judas, I want to see the city?"

"Me too please,"... that from Bartimaeus who by now had latched onto Jesus' company like a leech….. *"I've not seen it either." (with a grin)*

So, the three musketeers set out. In order to treat them to a full tour of the city, Judas took them up and in through the Sheep Gate at the northeast corner of the

---

[27] Biblical Passover meal

city next to Fortress Antonia. From there they ambled down the center of town *(called the 'Valley of the Cheesemakers')* north to south, sight-seeing as well as keeping their eyes out for an inexpensive site to hold their Seder meal. Judas explained that he didn't want them to celebrate in either a trashy, or expensive touristy place. The nicest section of the city was the quiet law-abiding up-scale southwest corner where a lot of the priests lived, down near the Essene gate *(see page 4).* Fortunately, it was there that they lucked-up and found a suitable upper room that could accommodate all of them. Judas was unsuccessfully haggling over the price when Nathaniel happened to mention that it was for the Galilean prophet Jesus. After that, the enthusiastic innkeeper gave the whole thing to them at a rock bottom discounted price. This included the meal of lamb, olives, bitter herbs, fish sauce, unleavened bread, dates, and decent wine. Pleased with themselves, they then split up; Nathaniel and Elon going off like tourists to explore the city, leaving Judas to conduct *".....some unfinished business"*. They would meet back in Bethany,

Judas had heard from one of the Pharisee's servants who was a secret Zealot, that the Zealot's master Rubin was offering a substantial monetary reward to anyone who knew where he could meet privately and quietly with Jesus. As it happened, Rubin's address was nearby. Now Judas wasn't born yesterday. He rightfully assumed it was a trap to get their hands on the Master. But no trap or person could overcome Jesus' power, and money was money…..and they were low on funds. So, Judas thought it would be fun and ironic to screw the bastards out of their money to help finance the very person they were stupid enough to try and execute. The idea appealed to his Zealot sense of justice. Besides, quite a few people knew Jesus' whereabouts these nights, and someone else was bound to turn him in to collect the reward, so why not him?

He figured it this way. When they came to arrest him, the first person to lay a hand on him would probably be struck blind, or dead. Either would be nice. Judas had personally witnessed him raising Lazarus, curing lepers, giving sight to blind men, feeding crowds from nothing, and the like. On top of all that, there had been that terrible storm at sea which he appeared to have calmed, although that was probably just a freak of the weather. In any case, the Master unquestionably had tremendous powers and could obviously strike down anyone he might wish to. But what was troubling Judas was why Jesus never cured his own headaches, toothaches, diarrhea and such? Why was that?! Was it possible that he could only work miracles for others? Or, what if they tried to imprison, or scourge him and for some illogical reason he simply let them? Judas was faced with a paradox. The Master seemed to be two different persons There was the *God-*

like Jesus who worked wonders and prophesied, and the *man-like* Jesus who bled, got sick, became tired and discouraged, who worried, and could be afraid and uncertain. Which one would be the Jesus they arrested?

The servant brought Judas in to Rubin's presence.

"Yes?"

"I've been told you're interested in the whereabouts of the prophet Jesus."

"Yes, I wish to meet the man privately to discuss a spiritual matter. Why, can you arrange for us to meet?"

"I'm sure I can bring you to him, but whether or not he'll wish to discuss your 'spiritual problem', is another matter. But I can bring you to him. I understand there is a reward. If so, what is it?"

"Thirty pieces of silver, but only if I get to see him before Passover."

"Rumor has it that the High Priest intends to have this Jesus condemned. This isn't perchance your 'spiritual matter' is it?"

"That's none of your concern unless you wish to share the Nazarene's fate as well. Just give me the information I require and keep your mouth shut, and all will be well for you. But betray us, and we'll hunt you down and have you crucified along with him and anyone else who interferes. ***Do I make myself clear?!****"*

At the mention of his own crucifixion, Judas began to sweat! Over the years, he had often had nightmares of his friend Eben-Ezar's horrible death *(see page 9)*. He should have known better than to ever have come here and think he could deal with these people. Now damnit he was in over his head. He suddenly desperately needed to visit a toilet. He tried to back out.

"Oh don't worry about me, I was merely curious. My information is probably uncertain anyway, so I'll be going. Sorry to have troubled you."

"Guard!" *(an armed man appeared). "You're not going anywhere! You'll do exactly as I say and lead me to him....that is if you wish to continue breathing our Judean air, which I understand is rather difficult when hanging from your wrists out there on Golgotha. I certainly hope I'm making myself clear. Now speak up, when and where shall we meet, for you to lead me to him.* ***Come on, out with it, or I'll have this guard take you away this very instant!!"***

Since the son-of-a-bitch put it that way, what choice did he have? Judas desperately wished he had remained with Nate and Elon showing them the city.

"Well, if you insist, be at the Dung Gate tomorrow night, after the Seder, let's say around the fifth hour (11 p.m.). But I think I should warn you. This Jesus has great powers and if he wishes, with a mere flick of his hand, he might turn you into a blind man or a small heap of ashes."

"Don't make me laugh. If he tries anything, he'll regret it and that goes for any of you fools who might try and interfere. We've dealt with cheap trickster

magicians before and they've all ended up begging to die quickly."

"What about the money?"

"You'll get it, when I get him. ***Now, get out of here!"***

Judas couldn't resist taking a *'Parthian shot'*[28] at this arrogant bastard,

"Fine, but don't complain to me later when you're a pillar of salt!"....and he was passed out the door before the guard could hit him.

Once safely out on the crowded street, Judas became furious, first with himself, and next with the bastard he had just left. He had done it again! It seemed like every time he tried to accomplish something worthwhile in his life, it had turned to ****! Well, these priests and elders asked for it, and were now going to get it in spades..... this time they weren't playing with any trickster. This time by damn, they would be paying thirty denarii for their own funerals! He dared not tell either the Master or any of the eleven, what had happened. They'd never understand his motives. Perhaps Levi or Shim might, but he couldn't take that chance. The important thing was that afterward when the Master was victorious, they'd all clap him on the back, and thank him for risking his neck, even old Sour Puss.

---

[28] When the Parthians fled a battlefield, they'd turn in their saddle and fire one last arrow at the Romans.

As he walked back up the hill to Bethany, he had this uncomfortable feeling that things just might *'go south' (i.e. go wrong).*

****

The following evening, Jesus and the twelve trooped down the Kidron Valley around the southeast corner of the city, past the Dung Gate and up in through the Essene Gate. In that way along with the help of nightfall, they managed to avoid attracting any attention. The women and others remained behind to celebrate the Seder in family style with Lazarus and his sisters.

The traditional evening started with the washing of the hands and a hymn. Next, Jesus had Levi read from Exodus. Then just before the meal began, Jesus arose from his couch, removed his outer clothing, and wrapped a towel around his waist. Then, pouring water into a basin, he knelt at Simon's feet,

"What are you trying to do?!"

"What does it look like? I'm going to wash your big feet."

"Look, you're the Master. You can't go around washing my feet. What would people think? Here, gimme that towel and basin. I'll wash yours."

Jesus stifled a growl. *"For heaven's sake Peter, am I ever going to be able to do anything without you objecting? I'm trying to give the twelve of you a lesson in humility by washing all your dirty feet. There are no bigshots in my kingdom. All of us are servants. Will you guys ever get that? Now, for once Peter, shut the heck up and gimme your ugly foot!"*

Little Jim stuck in his two cents worth that got them laughing,

"Master, if you're gonna wash our feet, for heaven's sake please make sure you do Shim's last. They really smell and it might be catching."

"Amen." ….that from Thaddeus who rarely said much.

When done washing all twelve, he straightened up, put back on his clothes, and resumed dinner and chatting.

Partway through the meal, he became quite serious.

"As you know, since time immemorial, we Jews, have offered sacrifices of our best lambs and animals, asking the Father for the remission of our sins. As I've told you on three previous occasions, in the next day or so, out of love for you, I will allow myself to be sacrificed for the forgiveness of the sinfulness of man."

Taking a loaf of bread, he broke it into thirteen pieces, blest it, then lifting his eyes towards his father in heaven, gave it to them saying,

"Take this and eat it, for this is my body which I will be giving up for you and all mankind."

After that, he took a quart pitcher of wine and again blest it, and lifting his eyes to the Father said to them,

"Drink this. It is my blood of a new covenant, which will be shed for you and all men for the forgiveness of sin in the world."

He went on.

"Henceforth, I want you to repeat this in memory of me. Don't misunderstand me. When hereafter you do this, the bread and wine you consecrate will indeed be me, and not some symbolism, but the real me. It is the Father's and my gift to you. When a man gives a gift to someone he loves, it becomes an intimate bond they then share between them. With this gift of my body and blood, each time you do this, I will become part of you, and you of me. I know it is impossible for you to comprehend, but accept it as a mystery of your faith in me."

This wasn't the first time they had heard him talking this shocking business about drinking his blood.....about cannibalism. They couldn't grasp the concept especially because of what it clearly says in the Torah prohibiting consuming blood.

> **"Moreover, you shall eat no blood whatever, whether of fowl or of animal, in any of your dwellings. Whoever eats any blood, that person shall be cut off from his people."**

So, they were understandably confused. Indeed, it was a matter of faith. Not knowing what to say, they said nothing.

After the meal, he brought up something else that was also startling.

"I have a secret source in the Sanhedrin who has informed me that one of you is going to betray me for reward money."

They all looked at each other except for Andrew who glared at Judas. Jesus then leaned towards Judas and quietly inquired,

"You wouldn't happen to know who this is would you Judas?"

Judas almost became sick. How was he going to explain what he had done? So, not knowing what to say, he lied in a mumble,

"I…aaaah…I have no idea Master,"

At the end of the meal, they sang the traditional *Hallel (benediction)*,

"♫Praised art Thou, O Lord, King of the Universe, who hast redeemed us, and hast redeemed our fathers from Egypt."

No one other than Jesus noticed that Judas was no longer in the room.

Chapter 11

(Arrest)

It was well into the night, perhaps the fourth hour *(10 pm)* when they thanked the owner of the upper room and went out into the night, retracing their steps out of the city. It was about a twenty-minute walk back up the Kidron Valley to the garden of the gethsemane *(olive press)* where Jesus often went at night to be by himself to meditate and pray. It was the only part of his long stress-filled busy day that he had a little peace and quiet, away from all the nastiness of the Pharisees and petty squabbling of his retinue. While he prayed, the others would each find a comfortable spot, wrap himself in his robe and generally doze. This night he prayed begging not to have to undergo crucifixion. But like with many of our prayers, the Father doesn't always seem to answer them, or at least not the way ignorant **'we'** think best! So, it was with *'the man'* Jesus. Around the sixth hour *(midnight).* Simon was aroused by a large group of noisy men approaching up the valley road carrying torches. By the time they arrived, Jesus and the others were all up and alert. Andrew was the first to recognize who was leading the pack.

*"Look! It's that ******* Judas!"*

There were twenty or thirty of the newcomers, many of whom could be seen carrying either swords or cudgels.

(Jesus in Gethsemane by Fuchs)

Judas walked up to Jesus and gave him a hug, whispering in his ear,

"*Master,they made me do this. They intend to arrest and later kill you! So strike them down now. Turn them blind or if you want, kill them!*"

"*Judas, since when do I need you to tell me what to do? You should never have done this, but it's what my Father apparently wants, so, so be it.*"

Rubin who was the leader of the mob, ordered,

"Grab this man and tie his hands. ***The rest of you people hear this! Anyone who interferes with my arresting this man, will be hunted down and receive the same punishment as he does. Do I make myself clear?!"***

Now the servants and Temple guards knew they were dealing with a powerful sorcerer. They all had heard exaggerated stories of his miracles. In fact, most of the guards were familiar with the blind beggar from the Temple. They weren't idiots. Let someone else be the first to grab this guy and maybe be turned into a black cat or a stone! But when a furious Rubin threatened,

"Do you all have trouble hearing? I told you to grab him! Do it now or I'll have all your yellow asses tonight in our dungeon!"

With that, they tentatively closed in. A couple of the frightened servants began clumsily manhandling Jesus trying to tie his hands behind his back. Simon, Big Jim and two of the other five Bethsaida fishermen were in the front ranks along with Shim. The others, unfamiliar with physical confrontations, hung nervously back in the flickering shadows cast by the flaming torches. It was about then that the slugfest ensued. Big Jim triggered the melee when he hauled off and took a mighty swing at the jaw of the poor fellow standing nearest the Jesus. At that, the Pharisee leader Rubin yelled out,

"Arrest them all! Arrest them all!"

Initially, it was only with fists.....that is until pugnacious Simon almost turned it into a bloodbath. He pulled out the long fisherman's knife he always carried at night and took a swipe at one of the servants trying to tie up Jesus. With all the wrestling on the part of the man grabbing Jesus, the blade ended up glancing off the poor fellow's skull, leaving his[29] left ear dangling by a thread. Dropping Jesus' arm, he doubled over grabbing the loose ear howling in pain, that is until Jesus reached down with his now free arm and gently touched the ear which instantly was healed. With that first show of a lethal weapon, the soldiers all drew their swords. Now the fishermen of the group were familiar with donnybrooks *(free-for-all brawls)*. The others however were about as useful in a fight as tits on a boar-hog. But they weren't fools. Over a dozen soldiers had drawn their weapons, and all the eleven had were Simon and Big Jim's two knives. It was either *'He that fights and runs away, will live to fight another day'*, or probably die right there in the dark, and they weren't ready for martyrdom, at least not that night.....so they ran! In fact, Levi, Didymus, Little Jim, Thaddeus, and Nathaniel had already taken off into the trees as fast as their legs would carry them. Because of the dark and confusion, they all somehow luckily escaped unscathed except for John Boy so to speak. Two soldiers trying to grab him ending up with only handfuls of his clothing.

[29] Caiaphas' servant named Malchus who later became a follower of the risen Jesus

John managed to escape, running like a deer, unencumbered by anything more than his flapping loincloth!

As they led him away, Jesus saw someone jumping up and down in the background of the crowd waving his hands. It was Judas. He seemed to be silently mouthing,

"STRIKE! STRIKE! NOW! NOW!".

The first part of Judas' plan had worked, he had the money, but the second part wasn't happening! The Master for whatever stupid reason was allowing them to lead him meekly away like a sheep going to the slaughter. What the hell was he up to? Judas couldn't understand it.

Jesus' loyal flock had scattered in twos and threes like quail, off amongst the olive trees into the night in every different direction. Now subject to arrest, they were afraid to return to Bethany, all except John Boy who had no choice. being naked. Simon didn't run far. Finding himself alone, and feeling ashamed, he turned back and in the dark, cautiously tailed the mob back down around the city and up to the house of the High Priest. That left Judas standing completely alone in the garden of the gethsemane, with only the sound of a lone cricket to break the tranquil silence. A slight movement behind some bushes caught the corner of his eye. He quietly called out,

"It's me Judas. Come out."

With that, Nathaniel and the two formerly blind men

(Caiaphas)

Elon and Aryeh, cautiously stepped out. Ever since Jesus cured them, the two had tagged along wherever Jesus went. Nathaniel was the first to speak.

"Judas what the hell is going on? What in heaven's name have you done?"

"First we'd better get away from here before somebody comes back."

He led them off up the slope of the Mount of Olives to a quiet, secluded, grassy spot where they sat down and wrapped themselves in their robes to keep out the early morning chill. It was there that Judas explained his plan that had gone awry. He ended his defense by appending,

"I still can't understand why he didn't strike them dead or blind right then and there. It baffles me.".....then a thought occurred to him,

"Ya know Nate, maybe he's waiting until he's got the whole lot of them together before he strikes, What do you think?"

"I surely hope so! I must say Judas, that's the dumbest plan I ever heard of. You realize you might end up getting us all killed. What the hell were you thinking?"

"Yeah, I guess you're right. I wish now I'd never gone to them, although someone else in the city certainly would've."

"Did he give you the money?"

"Yeah, but I wish he hadn't."

(Aryeh:) *"Ya know, this was the first fight I've ever seen. Being a follower of the Master apparently is going to be exciting."*

That last innocent observation calmed them all down enough to let them fall into troubled slumber. The new day promised to be exciting.

****

In the meanwhile, John had run nonstop to Bethany. He needed clothes. The women were all long since asleep, but Lazarus the host was dozing, awaiting the return of Jesus. He was awakened by a faint tapping at the door. When he went to investigate, there stood John shivering and as naked as a jaybird.

"John! What in heaven's name happened to you? Where are the others? Come in, come in. Where are your clothes?"

"Quick, can you please lend me some clothes? They're coming after me! I need to hide! The Master was arrested and some of the others too. When they tried to grab me, I wrestled out of my clothes and ran. I need to hide, quick!"

"First some clothes, then calm down and tell me everything."

By the time the excited, frightened young man had finished his story, his mother Salome and the other women were up and listening. Lazarus arranged for John to spend the night up on his neighbor's roof. No one would think of looking there. Once John was gone, young Mary announced,

"First thing in the morning, I'm going down into the city to find out what's happened to the Master."

Jesus' mother added, *"Mary, you're not going by yourself. I'll go with you."*

The other two mothers said they would go as well.

Chapter 12

(before Pilate)

The first thing the next morning upon awakening, Lazarus fetched down John and they all had a brief breakfast. As the women prepared to depart, John inquired,'

"Where are you going? What about me?! They'll come looking for me!"

Salome replied,

"You're coming with us. We need a man along in case any of that crowd tries to get molest us or young Mary"

"But Mom...."

"No more 'But Mom's'. You're going, and bring your walking stick just in case."

"Mom, you might be getting me killed ya know!"

"Well. better a dead lion for a son, than a live donkey. Let's go."

****

At this same time, Judas and his companions were also awake and up. He warned them to stay out of sight while he went in to reconnoiter the city and find out what was happening to Jesus. Nathaniel was worried,

"Where can we hide. That man said we were to be hunted down and punished."

Aryeh replied. *"Don't worry Nate, we'll hide out at my mom and dad's. They can't stand those pompous priests, especially after they questioned them about me."*

Judas went on,

"That's a great idea, but be careful going into the city. Avoid the Temple area and the Upper City (Mount Zion on the west side where many of the priests and Levites lived). Go in through the Dung Gate and mix with the crowds shopping along the Cheesemakers Valley. And Nate, whatever you do, let these guys do the talking. One word out of you and everyone within hearing will know you're from Galilee!"

Judas' first stop was across the street from Rubin's house where he was told by a servant that the Nazarene had been taken first to Annas'[30] house, then to Caiaphas's. The last thing the servant knew was that this morning his master said they were taking the Galilean to see the Procurator.

By the time Judas arrived outside Fortress Antonia, it was approaching the sixth hour *(noon)*. A fierce sun was beating down irritating a rowdy crowd, mostly of priests, Pharisees, and their servants. They seemed to be waiting for something. Judas inquired of a man standing next to him,

"What's going on? What is everyone standing around for?"

---

[30] Annas was former High Priest, and Caiaphas' father-in-law

"We brought the Galilean trickster here earlier for the Procurator to condemn, but the slimy Roman has been trying to weasel out of it. He's been trying to let him go. He went back in an hour ago and hasn't come back out."

Looking across the noisy crowd Judas spotted a worried-looking John with his headdress half-covering his face. With him were *'the Marys'*....Jesus' mom, *'the Magdalene'*, John Boy's mom Salome, and Shim's mom. Good for them! They sure had guts. He started shouldering his way in their direction when suddenly the mob hushed as a small, clean-shaven, short-haired, fiftyish looking man in a toga came out on the porch and held up his hand for silence. It was apparently the Procurator. Behind him supported by two soldiers was a tall man, face battered, with some sort of odd ugly crown on his head and wearing a purple robe. Judas groaned. It was the Master.

Pilate spoke in hesitant Aramaic.

"Behold the man!"

With that he had the soldier pull off the robe and show the crowd Jesus' back. Judas gasped in horror. The Master's entire back and buttocks had the appearance of chopped liver.

"Look, I am bringing him out to you to let you know that I find no basis for a charge against him."

If Pilate thought the planed scourging would engender sympathy from the crowd, he was greatly mistaken. Instead, it seemed to do just the opposite.

Led by the priests the mob began to chant in Latin in unison over and over,

"Crucifigerent! *(crucify him)* ***"Crucifigerent!"***

(Jesus and Pilate)

Pilate tried to speak but they drowned him out chanting even louder. He hated these priests. His sources in Rome had informed him that the Sanhedrin had gone behind his back to Emperor Tiberias complaining that he was inciting riots with his administration. Their backstabbing could cost him his job *(and it eventually did).* He finally gave up. Judas watched as he ceremoniously washed his hands of the entire mess and gave Jesus to them for crucifixion. During the washing, Jesus' and Judas' eyes had met, Judas frantically made exaggerated chopping motions with his arm implying ***"Strike! Strike!"*** but the person he loved most in the world merely sadly shook his head and was led away. Judas was stunned. Where the hell were all those thousands of supporters who were cheering for him just four days earlier? Where the hell were they?!

(Pilate)

With that, Judas took off sobbing as he blindly ran clutching his bag of silver. He ran to where the Sanhedrin met, in a fruitless attempt give back the money and save his beloved Master, but to no avail. They just laughed at him. He went out and blindly headed south across the city towards the Essene Gate, cursing, sobbing, and incoherently babbling as he went, like someone demented.

****

It was a little after the ninth hour that the tears were wiped away from Judas' eyes when Jesus welcomed him into his arms.

Epilog

(The victor gets to write the history books)

On that dreadful day, all but John deserted Jesus. They ran with their tails between their legs and hid in various homes cowering in fear, while their Master went to his ignominious death. In addition to that, Simon even publicly denied him more than once. Even three days later, it was only the fearless Magdalene who had the guts to go to the tomb. The rest of them remained hidden in dark attics and cellars.

Thus it was, that many years later when some of them wrote or narrated their memoirs, they perhaps subconsciously needed a handy scapegoat to take the focus off their own cowardice and betrayals.....**and who better than the dead Judas?** Nobody ever liked him anyway. He wasn't one of them, a Galilean. Not only that, he was an unfriendly loner and penny-pinching miser....some even thought, a thief. Fortunately for them, they were the ones dictating the gospel accounts!

What happened to them according to tradition?

Peter: crucified, Rome, ±64AD, 33 years after Jesus. age ±63

Andrew: Crucified, Patras, Greece ±65AD, age ±62

James: beheaded, Jerusalem, ±44AD, 11 years after Jesus, age ±38

John: died Ephesus, Turkey ±100AD age ±93

Philip: crucified, Hierapolis, Turkey, ±80AD age ±75

Bartholomew: crucifixtion, Albanopolis, Armenia, age ±68

Matthew: stoned or beheaded, Sebastopolis, Turkey, ±74AD, age ±69

Thomas: lanced, Chennai, India, ±72AD age ±67

James: stoned, Jerusalem, 5 years after Jesus, age ±32

Simon: beheaded, Beirut. Syria, ±65 AD, age ±60

Jude: beheaded, Beirut, Syria, ±65 AD, age ±60

END

The message is that if Jesus welcomed home repentant Judas, then if we are truly sorry, he'll welcome you and me no matter what stupid things we might have ever done.

(apologies to Levi, Mark, Luke and John Boy)

Made in the USA
Columbia, SC
09 July 2022

62906748R00068